Life, Love, and the Pursuit of Free Throws

ALSO BY JANETTE RALLISON

All's Fair in Love, War, and High School

Life, Love, AND

THE Pursuit OF

Free Throws

Janette Rallison

SCHOLASTIC INC.

New York   Toronto   London   Auckland   Sydney
Mexico City   New Delhi   Hong Kong   Buenos Aires

ISBN 0-439-75426-7

12 11 10 9 8 7 6 5 4 3 2 1   5 6 7 8 9 10/0

Printed in the U.S.A.   40

First Scholastic printing, February 2005

All the characters and events portrayed in this work are fictitious, with the exception of Rebecca Lobo, who has agreed to and approved her cameo appearance in this work.

Book design by Jennifer Ann Daddio

To all my friends, past and present, who make life a fun place.

Especially to Lorell Morrell and Leslie Thompson,

who've been bringing me laughter for the last

seventeen years, and to Laura Kleinhofs, who shared

those crazy teen years with me. We told strangers

we were orphans in order to get newspaper

subscriptions, tricked our boss into taking us

to Baskin-Robbins, were responsible for

various toilet-papering jobs, and nearly got

stranded at a gas station in Seattle.

Ahh, those were the days.

Special thanks to Rebecca Lobo for her cameo in the novel.

One

Josie

There are three times in life when it's important not to trip: when you're going for the tie-breaking layup in a basketball game, when you're walking down the aisle on your wedding day, and when your English teacher asks you to hand out textbooks—and you're about to give one to Ethan Lancaster.

I knew this. I actually thought about it as I was walking toward him, which is probably what doomed me. It's like typing. I can do it if I don't think about it. As soon as I start to think about where my fingers are placed on the keyboard, I create words that look like space-alien vocabulary.

> CAMI'S LAST IM TO ME: Hey, Josie. How's it going?
> ME: Really hppf smf upi.

Ever since I started my freshman year I've tried to create an image of sophistication and mystique to impress Ethan, to have it all ruined in one day.

Two feet away from his desk, I tripped. My entire armful

of *American Poetry: A Viewpoint* went flying into the air. I think one may have hit Ethan, but I'm not sure, because by then my viewpoint was an extreme close-up of the floor. I was just doing my best not to roll under Ashley Holt's desk.

Everyone in the class stopped talking and stared at me. Mrs. Detwiler shuffled over to help me up, which was a good thing, since all Ashley did was look down at me. Ashley is good at looking down at people, so this shouldn't have surprised me.

Mrs. Detwiler helped me to my feet. Her lips pressed together in a frown. "Are you all right?"

"Yeah, I'm fine." Or at least I would be when everyone stopped staring at me. The stinging in the palms of my hands and the pain in my side were probably not permanent things.

"You need to be more careful, or you're going to hurt yourself."

Right. Thank you, Mrs. Detwiler. I would have never come to that conclusion by myself. I was planning on incorporating a backflip into my next walk across the classroom, but on second thought . . .

I reached down and began picking books up off the floor. You'd think since everyone had just witnessed my spectacular dive, the people around me would offer to help me.

They didn't.

All the kids nearby sat in their seats watching me like they were waiting to see if I had enough coordination to walk and pick up books at the same time. Perhaps they were checking to see if I was about to make a tripping encore.

Mrs. Detwiler picked up a few books and went to the

next aisle to pass them out. Cami came from the other side of the room to help me pick up the rest. She handed a couple of them out to the students around us but didn't give one to Ethan.

She knows I have a thing for him.

I walked up to him again, a book in my outstretched arm.

"I already have one," he said. "I picked up one that slid under my desk."

"Oh."

I passed out the remaining books, then retreated to my desk to listen to Mrs. Detwiler's lecture about our new poetry unit.

I didn't dare look at Ethan. I didn't dare look at anyone. Mrs. Detwiler droned on about assonance and alliteration, and how when she was in school students were required to memorize pages of poetry, and she could still recite Edgar Allan Poe's "The Raven" word for word. And then she did—staring at us wide eyed and occasionally waving one hand around for emphasis.

She finished the poem with a smug smile, even though I could see no conceivable advantage to memorizing pages of poetry when you can look up anything online. I mean, if by some chance you were ever walking around thinking, Hey, I sure would like to read a poem about spooky ravens, you probably could find a whole flock of them at birdpoetry.com.

Still, Mrs. Detwiler told us we not only had to memorize poems, we had to write three poems about ourselves by the end of the month and recite one of them.

There was a collective groan from the class, which only made Mrs. Detwiler click her tongue as though we'd severely disappointed her. "If I could do it in the ninth grade, so can you. And who knows, perhaps when you're forty, you'll still remember it."

Actually, I was hoping my teenage memories would have little to do with poetry. I would rather remember being suddenly popular, indispensable to the basketball team, and having a conversation with Ethan that didn't happen after I took a nosedive in front of his desk.

As Mrs. Detwiler went on about the power of poetry, one thought ran through my mind. What did I have to do—how could I change myself into someone Ethan liked?

Cami

After basketball practice, Josie and I did our homework at my house and then went outside to shoot some more hoops. As we played, Josie talked about Ethan (as usual), and I talked about Rebecca Lobo's visit in a month (as usual).

Rebecca Lobo has been my idol since I started playing basketball at age eight. She's retired from the WNBA now, but I still think she's the greatest. When she ran down the court, it looked like the basketball was a part of her, as though she didn't have to think to play.

Rebecca was also an old college friend of our freshman coach, Mrs. Melbourne. The coach is very proud of the fact that they played together in Connecticut, and she has two Rebecca Lobo posters and a framed Connecticut Sun shirt in her office. The coach also tells us Rebecca stories and Rebecca updates, and since Rebecca is coming to Phoenix for a vacation this winter, Coach Melbourne made her promise to drive out to Sanchez for a visit.

Coach Melbourne has had an extra strut in her walk ever since. She got Rebecca to agree to speak to the audience at halftime about the importance of girls' sports programs. But the really wonderful thing is this—Rebecca said she'd run some basketball drills using a girl from each team to help her demonstrate.

Coach Melbourne said our team's MVP would have the honor. We all figured that meant the highest-scoring player.

There are very few girls on the team who can outshoot me. Josie is one of them.

I dribbled the ball, taking small steps that led me nowhere, waiting for the right moment to rush past Josie for a layup. "In thirty-four days one of us could be doing this with Rebecca Lobo." *Dribble. Dribble.* "Do you suppose the WNBA recruits fourteen-year-olds? We could drop out of high school and take up a career as fabulously wealthy celebrity athletes."

Josie stood in front of me with her arms stretched out, but hardly seeing me. "I should have turned the whole thing into a joke. I should have looked up at Ethan and said, 'Well, another girl has fallen for you.' I mean, if you can laugh at yourself, people think you're cool. Otherwise you just look like a klutz." She cocked her head. "Do you think Ethan thinks I'm a klutz?"

"I think Ethan has forgotten the whole thing. And speaking of forgetting, don't let me forget to bring my video camera when Rebecca comes. I want to make sure someone records Rebecca and me playing together."

"Right, Camilla."

With the exception of my grandmother, Josie is the only person who calls me Camilla. She says it's a pretty name, so I don't stop her.

I rushed down to the basket, jumped, and shot. The ball hit the backboard and ricocheted to Josie. She dribbled back to half-court, laughing. "Don't get your camera out yet."

I put my arms out, guarding her. "I'll make the next one."

"Maybe, but I'll still be the team's high scorer because you can't sink a free throw to save your life."

This was not exactly true. If my life depended on it, I'd probably be able to make a free throw.

Josie pivoted around me, took four steps toward the basket, and produced a perfect layup.

I dribbled the ball back to the white painted line on the driveway that represented the free-throw line. I concentrated, aimed—already making the shot in my mind. Unfortunately, that was the only place I made the shot. The ball hit high on the backboard and bounced down to Josie. She walked over next to me, tossed the ball toward the basket, and smiled as it swished through.

"Teach me how to do that," I said.

Josie shrugged. "You point. You shoot. What's there to teach?"

Which was the really annoying thing about Josie. Her basketball skill didn't come from practice, it just happened. The ball liked her better.

I worked harder. I'd been playing longer. In fact, I was the one who got Josie involved in basketball in the first place. I made her start shooting hoops with me back in the sixth grade after my former best friend, Ashley Holt, and I stopped speaking to each other.

And Josie was better than I was.

I went and grabbed the ball, walked it back to the free-throw line, and took another shot. It bounced once on the rim, then fell off the basket and rolled into the bushes.

"It isn't fair," I said. "I have posters of Rebecca Lobo all over my bedroom wall. What do you have on your wall?"

"Mostly fingerprints."

"I watched every game she was in, and you watched her games when?"

"When there wasn't something better on."

I tossed up my hands. "Do you see my point?"

Josie went and grabbed the ball from the bushes. "So what do you want me to do about it? Miss shots on purpose so you have a better chance at MVP?"

"Yes. You could also feed the ball to me more, and help me work on my free throw after practice."

"I can't do that very often. I've got homework to do. And besides, I've decided to take up shopping." She said this as though it were a new religion.

"Shopping for what?"

"Clothes. I need a new image, one Ethan will notice. Right now I have no flair. No pizzazz. Ashley has designer everything."

Ashley also had streaked blond hair, the body of a swim-suit model, and a face straight off a Barbie doll. She could have worn nothing but old newspapers held together with Scotch tape, and she would have received more attention from guys than the rest of us in school.

You couldn't compete with Ashley; you just had to settle for the leftovers in the guy department. Personally, I put guys into two categories. The guys who are Ashlified—meaning they have recently dated, are dating, or hope to be dating Ashley, and thus consider the rest of us not up to their stan-dard—and the regular guys.

Ethan was definitely Ashlified. He and Ashley were the constant on-again, off-again item. Plus Josie idolized Ethan, so he was off-limits to me, even if he did have thick, wavy brown hair, gorgeous blue eyes, and a locker so close to mine that I saw him every day. He usually came by while I was get-ting my books out before first period, and I would position myself in front of my locker, shifting things back and forth on the shelf while I watched him out of the corner of my eye.

Sometimes he smiled at me, and when he did, I always smiled back, but I never told Josie that. She wouldn't under-stand. Well, actually—she *would* understand, and probably hate me for it.

The problem was, I hadn't started out liking Ethan. At first he was just that good-looking but annoyingly arrogant boy Josie liked. Now somehow he'd become ultra-good-looking—so good-looking that the arrogant thing just seemed natural.

Who wouldn't be arrogant when they were handsome, popular, and had been captain of both the freshman football and basketball teams?

Every time he was around, I suddenly became acutely aware of how I was standing, what I was saying. I worried if my hair was in place or my mascara was smeared. I wanted him to notice me but then hoped he wouldn't.

I'd been Ethanized.

Around Josie, I went out of my way to pretend I didn't like him. If I acted like I didn't like him, then eventually it would be the truth. Crushes were temporary things, like the flu. You just had to live through them.

I shrugged at Josie and held the basketball under the crook of my arm. "You don't need to spend your time shopping. Ethan is a guy. He won't notice what you wear unless it's made from wild animals, is covered with the answers to the next algebra test, or is on fire."

"But Ashley wears—"

"Girls wear nice clothes to impress other girls. Guys don't notice those things. Trust me, I have an older brother. Save your money and help me work on my free throws. We'll both be happier."

"Maybe I should buy makeup then, or perfume, or change my hair." She pulled her long brown hair out of its ponytail. "Do you think I should get a perm?"

I double-bounced the ball while I thought. "You don't need to spend money on stuff to get Ethan to notice you. I can help you with that. I live with a guy, so I know how they think. Coach me on my free throws, and I'll coach you on Ethan."

Josie put her hand on her hip, but didn't outright question my abilities.

"I'll prove I know what I'm talking about." I motioned for Josie to follow me to my front porch. Once she got there, I opened the door, and we stepped into our family room. Kevin, my sixteen-year-old brother, was lying on the couch watching television and flipping potato chips into his mouth.

"Hey, Kevin, you know Diane, that girl you like?"

He didn't look away from the television. "Yeah."

"Did you see her today?"

"Yeah. So?"

"What color shirt did she wear?"

He snorted, then shoved another chip in his mouth. "I don't know."

"See," I told Josie. "Spend your time helping me practice free throws." I opened the front door to go out, but she hesitated in the family room, then took a step closer to Kevin. "What about her perfume? Did you notice what she smelled like? Or her eye shadow—was it the frosty kind, or the muted kind?"

Kevin glanced over his shoulder at us. "You two are so weird."

I took Josie's arm and pulled her from the room and back outside. After the front door was shut firmly behind us, I leaned up against it. "What did I tell you? I know how guys think."

"All right, if you understand guys, what do I need to do to get Ethan's attention?"

I held my hand out as though making a deal. "You help me on my free throws—help me get the MVP spot—and I'll help get Ethan to notice you."

Josie picked up the ball from where I'd left it on the porch and bounced it twice. "Notice me how? I mean, he noticed me today. He noticed that I fell on the ground."

"He'll notice you're beautiful, talented, and smart. I guarantee you'll have at least three conversations with him before Rebecca comes, or you can refuse to throw me the ball."

Josie reached out and shook my hand.

Which meant I had a shot at playing with Rebecca, or at least I would if I could get Ethan to talk to Josie.

Two

Josie

I thought about Ethan for the rest of the night—which was not out of the ordinary, except this time, as I pictured him sitting in class, his bangs falling across his forehead in that slightly mussed way, I wondered if what Cami said could be true.

Would I talk to him soon—not once, but three times?

We were about to pair up with partners in biology class to work on science projects. Was it wishing for the impossible to want Ethan to team up with me?

That night Cami e-mailed me a list of things I needed to get Ethan to notice me. Cami is one of those ultraorganized people who makes lists for everything. Her to-do list for me was

1. Smile while walking through the hallways at school.
2. Don't giggle nervously.
3. Don't slouch.
4. If you catch Ethan's eye, say, "Hi."

5. If he says, "Hi," back to you, try to start a
conversation.
6. Don't use the words *um, uh,* or *huh* in sentences.

Permitted things to say to Ethan:
Anything about sports, especially basketball.
Not permitted to say:
That your free-throw average is better than his.
Permitted to say:
How are you?
Not permitted to answer:
Madly in love with you.
Permitted to say:
Anything about his friends.
Not permitted to say:
Anything embarrassing about me.

Which just shows you how much confidence Cami has in
my conversational powers. Like, what was she afraid I would
say about her?

ME (while giggling and slouching): Hi, Ethan, have you
written a poem about yourself for English class yet?
ETHAN: No. Have you?
ME: Um, I'll probably do one about unrequited love.
Cami hasn't thought of anything to write yet though.
She, uh, has a hard time making up her mind sometimes.
ETHAN: Oh?
ME: Yeah, she's also a picky eater and an impulsive
shopper.

ETHAN: Really?

ME: And she was afraid of the dark until the third grade.

I mean, honestly, I do have some social graces. Still, I took Cami's list to heart.

The next day between classes I walked around school smiling. By fourth period my lips felt sore, and people kept glancing around the hallway to see what I was looking at.

I continued the grin during English class. Since Ethan was the reason for my big-teeth spotlight, I thought I shouldn't stop until he noticed me. He never looked my direction, but Mrs. Detwiler accused me of not paying attention.

Evidently she doesn't get a lot of students smiling while she recites Shakespeare's sonnets, and she figured if I looked happy, I must be doing something other than listening to her. (If only I could.)

After she scolded me, I put on my usual blank stare for the rest of English class. My lips enjoyed the rest. Then I smiled on the way to lunch, biology, and history.

Ethan never noticed the new, happier me, but I learned something important—there's a reason runway models don't smile while they walk down the catwalk. Mainly, you feel like an idiot strolling around smiling for no apparent reason. I'm sure this knowledge will come in handy if there's ever a shortage of runway models and they start drafting average-looking tall girls like me into the profession.

When school ended, Cami came by my locker. "Did you talk to Ethan today?"

"No."

"Well, don't get discouraged. This is only day one of our plan. Tomorrow we'll go outside to the courtyard where he and Justin hang out after lunch. And then we'll"—she fluttered one hand in the air—"we'll do something."

"What?"

"We'll talk to them." She pushed on my shoulder blades. "You're slouching again."

I straightened my back until my muscles strained.

"Now you're not smiling."

I smiled.

"And remember, don't giggle."

No chance of that. It was hard to laugh when both my lips and my back felt sore.

Guys. If only they knew what we went through for them.

Cami

The next day after lunch, Josie and I walked out to the courtyard to look for Ethan and Justin. We found them sitting on a bench eating their sack lunches.

I had no idea how to start a conversation with them, but I didn't let Josie know this. I was supposed to be the expert. I had to at least act like an expert if I wanted a chance to play with Rebecca Lobo.

You'd think after living with an older brother for fourteen years I'd know everything about guys, but my knowledge consisted of the following:

1. They think burping is hilarious.
2. They think sitting behind the wheel of a car gives them superpowers.
3. Punching each other is a form of communication.
4. They would rather shower standing in a brown tub every morning than clean the bathroom. This makes sense when you consider they like monster truck racing and football, two events that can't be done while staying clean. Dirt, apparently, is a guy thing.

That was all I knew about guys. I doubted any of it would help to get a conversation going with Ethan.

We sat down on the bench across the courtyard from him and Justin, and we talked about science projects, talked about nothing, really, because neither one of us was thinking about science.

I waited for an opportunity to—I didn't know what— bring up monster truck racing or toss out a compliment. *Hey, Ethan, you're pretty clean for a guy.*

Ethan threw a grape into the air and tried to catch it with his mouth while Justin said, "You'll never make it."

If only one of them would say something to us first. I mean, here we were, two girls by ourselves. . . .

We were pretty enough to attract attention, weren't we? Josie had smooth brown hair and dark eyes that gave her a mysterious look. Each year those features seemed more re-fined and feminine, as though she was a painting that was still getting the finishing touches.

I used to think I was the prettiest—guys are supposed to

like blonds best—but suddenly I wasn't sure. When Ethan looked over at us, who did he think was better looking?

"I wish you were in advanced biology with me, and we could do our science project together," Josie said. "We could think of something fun."

Josie was in all honors classes. I only had honors English, so I was in regular biology with all the other regular people. Which meant not only was Josie prettier than me. She was smarter too. Just like in basketball, I was number two.

My only advantage over her was that due to my older brother and his set of annoying friends, who constantly streamed through our house, I had more experience with guys. I had one advantage, and I was using it to help her attract the attention of the guy I liked.

"Of course I'd like to do my project with Ethan," Josie whispered, "but I can't even talk to him. I'd never be able to ask him to be my partner." She leaned in closer to me. "We're out here. What do we do next?"

Yes, what?

A grape bounced off Ethan's chin. As he made a grab for it, the sun streaked through his brown hair.

Justin took another grape from his lunch sack. "You're pitiful. Watch a pro." Justin threw the grape up in the air, and might have caught it in his mouth if Ethan hadn't pushed him out of the way. The grape hit Justin's cheek and then bounced to the ground. Justin picked up the grape and chucked it at Ethan. "You loser."

Ethan ducked and smiled. He had great teeth too.

The grape flew over toward our side of the courtyard, hit

the ground, and rolled under our bench. I picked it up. "You guys are both lousy shots. I'll show you how it's done." I took aim at the garbage can by Justin. "This is a three-pointer." I flung the grape, and it sailed toward the can, then plunked into the side of the can and dropped to the ground.

Justin snorted. "Not even close."

"Girls can't throw," Ethan said.

Josie tilted her head at him, all smiles. "Is that a challenge?"

"Nope, it's a fact Cami just demonstrated."

Her smile didn't falter. "I'm a better shot than Cami."

Which is just the thing you want your best friend to tell the guy you like.

"Prove it." Ethan tossed a grape to Josie.

She caught it with one hand, threw it into the air above her head, and opened her mouth. It fell onto her tongue, and she turned to Ethan, holding the grape between her teeth. "See."

"That was luck, not aim." Ethan tossed her another grape. "Try throwing it in my mouth."

She shook her head. "You'll cheat and move so it won't go in. If you want a contest, you throw one at Justin's mouth, I'll throw one at Cami's, and we'll see who has better aim."

"Fine." Ethan walked over to our bench, fingering a grape between his thumb and forefinger.

Josie pushed me toward Justin. "Come on, Camilla, this is one time when I need your big mouth over there."

Thanks. In the game of love, I had suddenly been reduced to a catcher's mitt with teeth.

I wanted her to miss.

Still, I stood unmoving beside Justin, my mouth hanging

open like I was preparing for a tonsillectomy. At the other bench Josie stared intently at me, the grape poised between her finger and her thumb. Her hand rocked back and forth as she took aim. Then with a flick of her wrist, she hurled the grape in my direction.

It was a good throw. Apparently, not only basketballs but also grapes liked Josie. She would make the shot, show Ethan she was dripping with talent, and gloat about it for the rest of the day.

If I tilted my chin down just a bit, she'd miss.

I kept my chin up, watching the grape soar toward me until it plopped into my mouth.

Josie held her hands up. "Victory!"

I wasn't sure whether to spit the grape out or eat it. I let it sit on my tongue in case Ethan demanded to see the proof.

He didn't. He just chucked his grape at Justin. The grape curved toward Justin's face but was too far to the left. Justin took a step in that direction, then straightened up, trying to center himself. He reminded me of one of those trained dolphins at Sea World who stand on their back fins to get food—except dolphins are better at it. The grape hit him in the forehead.

"Girls rule," Josie said.

"Rematch," Ethan said. "Best two out of three."

"All right," Josie said.

"Waid a minud." I held up a hand while I chewed the grape. It was bitter, and I tried not to purse my lips while I talked. "What if I don't want to stand here getting grapes thrown at my face?"

Ethan pulled two more grapes from his lunch bag and handed one to Josie. "Don't worry. She'll miss your face altogether next time."

Josie took aim. "You wish."

I barely had time to open my mouth before Josie tossed the next grape. It hit me on the nose, then fell to the ground.

"Ha!" Ethan said, then threw his grape at Justin.

Justin did another dolphinlike attempt trying to catch the grape, but missed.

Josie beamed. "I still win."

"Nope. It's two out of three. If you miss next time and I score, we'll be even and need to go to best three out of four."

"Do you have that many grapes?" Josie asked.

"We can pick the ones off the ground if we need to," he said.

"I'm not eating grapes off the ground," I called over to them.

"Of course you're not," Ethan called back. "She'll miss the rest of her shots."

But she didn't. She and Ethan threw three more times before the bell rang, and she landed a grape in my mouth twice. Ethan only got it in Justin's mouth once, and that was just because Justin was getting better at cheating.

"Best eight out of nine," Ethan called when the last round was over.

I walked back to the bench where my books were. "Sorry. We'll be late for class as it is."

Josie picked up her books, but didn't move away from Ethan. "At least you won't go to class hungry," she told me. "You got to eat grapes."

Yeah, but they were sour grapes.

I decided not to wait for Josie to pull herself away from Ethan. "I've got to go," I called over my shoulder, then walked back into the school. Our biology classes were in different directions, and besides, who knew how long she'd stand there flirting with Ethan. Any moment she'd ask him to be her science fair project partner, and he'd be thrilled.

I just didn't want to see it.

Josie

Justin looked at his watch and winced. "Mr. Renault will give me detention if I'm late again." He grabbed his books from the bench and headed out of the courtyard with quick steps.

I fiddled with my notebook paper, unsure whether I should wait to walk with Ethan to class, or whether that would be presumptuous. Now that I wasn't throwing grapes, I didn't know what to do with my hands.

Ethan picked up his books and glanced over at me. "Guess we'd better hurry, or Mr. Parkinson will make us clean out the lizard cages."

We walked silently out of the courtyard through one of the side doors and down the hallway to biology.

I should say something. Here was my chance to ask him to be my partner—the only chance I was likely to get, since we were choosing partners today in class.

The hallway was empty, and my footsteps echoed around me.

So, Ethan, would you be my science fair partner? That sounded like a marriage proposal. I'd have to come up with something more subtle. I switched my books from one hand to the other. "So, um, today's the day we're choosing partners in biology, right?"

Um. I'd said *um.* And I was probably slouching and not smiling.

Thirty seconds alone with Ethan, and I'd already broken three rules Cami had given me for impressing him. I straightened up and smiled, until I realized that smiling probably made me look like I loved biology.

"Yeah, today is the day," he said.

The bell rang. We were officially late. I didn't mind.

"Do you have any ideas about a project?" I asked.

"I was thinking of doing something on germs. Maybe test antibacterial soaps on different surfaces and see if they actually work."

"That's sounds interesting. So . . ." Would you be my partner? Only I couldn't say it. "So, um . . ." I'd said *um* again. This was getting worse. "So . . ." Why did I keep saying *so*? *So* was as bad as *um.* When Cami asked me how my first real conversation with Ethan went, I'd have to say, "It went so-so. Literally."

I cleared my throat. "I bet you'll do really well with germs." That sounded like an insult. I was lousy at talking with boys.

We rounded a corner, and the biology door came in sight.

"Maybe Parkinson won't notice we're late," Ethan said.

"Right." I knew he'd not only notice, he'd make a big

deal about marking us tardy and telling us we were disrupting class.

And then I smiled without forcing it. "They're probably choosing partners right now."

He didn't say anything.

"If everyone else is taken, I wouldn't mind doing something on germs."

We reached the door, and Ethan turned the knob. "Brendan and I already decided to be partners."

"Oh. Okay." I'm not sure he heard me. He walked through the door into the already jumbled classroom. Everyone was out of their seats, standing and talking in clusters of two. Some were congregated around a stack of science project books on Mr. Parkinson's desk.

Brendan came up to Ethan, notebook in hand. "There you are. I was afraid you were skipping class, and I'd be stuck with the Whine as my partner."

The Whine's real name was Frederick Vine, but he had earned the nickname due to years of complaining about everything at school. According to Frederick, the teachers graded unfairly, the popular kids got special treatment, and PE class was stupid. No one, he insisted, needs to know how to play badminton to succeed in life.

Well, yeah, but you don't see the rest of us complaining about all of it.

Mr. Parkinson stood behind his desk, looking over the top of his bifocals at Ethan and me. "Glad you two could fit class into your busy schedules. If you come in late again, you'll both have detention. Now choose a partner and get to work. You have until the end of class to decide on a project, write a paragraph describing it, and turn in a plan of action."

Ethan went off with Brendan, talking about petri dishes, without another glance in my direction.

I walked to my desk, looking around the room for a girl, any girl, who was still by herself.

No one.

I knew, but I still kept looking anyway. It wasn't until Frederick walked right up and plunked his books on my desk that I accepted the fact: I was stuck with the Whine.

Frederick was about five feet and nine inches, all of it knees and elbows. His dark brown hair was a little too long, as though he couldn't be bothered to cut it, and he usually walked like he was in a hurry to get somewhere. Maybe he was. I had never talked to him enough to find out.

He pulled a chair up to my desk, sat down, and opened up his notebook. "I wanted to work alone, but Mr. Parkinson says teamwork is part of the grade, so you can be my partner." He wrote "Description of Project" across the top of his paper. "We're going to test rocket stability with different fin configurations and balance."

I got out my own notebook. "Frederick, it's supposed to be a science project, not a NASA experiment."

He didn't stop writing. "This is exactly why I didn't want a partner. What kind of science project were you thinking of doing? Which nail polish stays on longer?"

"No," I said hotly, and then as I thought about it, "although at least that would be a useful thing to know."

"Rocket stability is a useful thing to know."

"Half the population wears nail polish. How many people launch rockets?"

Frederick continued writing his paragraph. "We're doing rocket stability. It will involve one day when we measure and weigh the rockets and another day when we launch them and track their trajectory. We'll also need to get the calculations to determine the center of pressure. I'm pretty sure we'll be able to get that off the Internet. I've already found a few sites to look at."

I tapped my pencil against my paper. "Wait a minute. This is supposed to be teamwork. How come you just get to decide what we're doing?"

"Because you think fingernail polish information is useful." He snorted and wrote in his notebook again. "What kind of idea could you come up with?"

"I can come up with a good idea." I leaned over to see what he was writing. It was a timetable of the rocket experiment we'd be doing and when we'd do the research.

He continued to write without looking at me. "And don't expect that I'll do everything, and you'll just put your name on it at the end. People think because I'm smart I'm going to let them cheat. Well, I won't."

I put one hand across his notebook. "Frederick, I think we're having a little teamwork problem. I'm still in the brain-storming-for-ideas phase of this project, and you've already decided it, planned it, and branded me a cheater."

"We're doing rocket stability."

"I'm not a cheater."

He pulled the notebook away from my hand. "I want to

get the project done before the regional chess tournament in two weeks so I can concentrate on that."

"Two weeks? Most people won't have even started procrastinating on their assignments by then."

"Yes, two weeks. It's stiff competition at State this year. I'll be up against Daniel 'the Knight Slayer' Dixon." He ripped out the sheet in his notebook and handed it to me. "This will be our schedule because I have chess club and debate on the other days."

"I have basketball practice after school every day until four fifteen."

He let out a tormented sigh. "Great. I'm stuck doing my science fair project with a jockette."

I handed his schedule back to him. "Just because I play sports doesn't mean I'm stupid. This is advanced biology. Everyone here is smart. You shouldn't just assume I'm a slacker."

He shrugged his shoulders. "If you're smart, and you're not a slacker, then rocket stability shouldn't be a problem for you."

"It wouldn't be."

"Good, because that's what we're doing our science project on."

"But—" But rocket stability sounded boring and hard. Only I couldn't tell him that after I'd just told him how smart and unslackerish I was. Now I was going to have to endure weeks of rocket calculations.

And really, I would have rather done a project on nail polish.

Three

Cami

I ran all the way to biology class and still came in two seconds after the bell rang. Most teachers would overlook two seconds, but not Ms. Brooks. The woman has had half a century to perfect the art of being mean, and she likes to use her skills on defenseless students. She hadn't even started taking roll yet, but she marked me tardy and assigned me a two-page report on the function of sodium chloride in the human body.

I walked to my desk, breathlessly. "But I don't even know what sodium chloride is. How am I supposed to find out its function?"

She tapped her pen against the roll book. "If you have problems, you can look it up in a dictionary, research it on the Internet, or just cry about it."

Several people in the class chuckled, although I didn't see what was so funny. Maybe it was just the nervous laughter of people who'd suddenly realized that (1) their biology teacher was deranged—we should have suspected as much from a woman who cut apart frogs year after year—and (2) this deranged woman had access to dangerous chemicals. I mean, how much of that frog-killing stuff did she have on hand?

I sat down at my desk silently, and Ms. Brooks shook her head as though disappointed in my intelligence. "Sodium chloride is salt, Cami. Salt is found in tears."

"Oh."

More laughter from the rest of the class.

Yes, thank you all. I was not only tardy, I was also the entertainment in today's biology class.

When Ms. Brooks finished with the roll, she assigned us science project partners. She assigned me Caroline Fipps, I assume, because she was still punishing me for coming in late.

Caroline was the only freshman I knew who wore acrylic nails. She also wore a ton of makeup and necklaces with strange symbols on them. If you sat near her at lunch, she'd tell you all about them. "This one's a druid symbol. It means love. This one's a Japanese word. It means mysterious."

What they actually meant was that she had no taste in jewelry.

And now—all because Josie couldn't stop playing grape toss with Ethan—Caroline was my science project partner.

Josie and Ethan were probably partners now, sitting close together in advanced bio, murmuring things like, "Let's do our project on chemistry. We have plenty of that."

Caroline scooted her chair over to my desk and laid her hands, today with light blue polish, across the top. "I already know what I want to do for our project—ESP."

I forced a smile at her. "It's supposed to be a science project. Psychic power stuff is not science."

She took her book bag from the floor, plopped it on the desk, and pulled out two books and a magazine. "*Discover* did an issue on Rupert Sheldrake. He studied the sixth sense—our ability to know when people are staring at us." She moved one hand across the air in front of me. "There you are sitting in class. Suddenly, for no reason, you look up and see someone staring at you. How did you know they were watching?" Both her hands and her eyebrows rose. "It's the sixth sense. We can duplicate Sheldrake's experiments and prove it exists."

"You want us to stare at people for our science project?"

She nodded. "That's the scientific method."

"I don't think Ms. Brooks will let us stare at people as a science project."

"Why not?"

"It's not science. That's like calling one of those psychic hotlines and asking them to predict things for us."

Caroline's eyes grew into wide circles. "What a good idea. We could document how often the psychic is right to prove people really do have ESP."

I leaned forward in my chair. "But people really don't have ESP."

She rolled her eyes, and I noticed she was wearing frosty blue eye shadow that matched her nails. "Well, not everybody. Only some people have the gift. I'm trying to develop my abilities so when I'm older I can get a job either as a fortune-teller or as a pet psychic."

"Um, great." I was stuck with a science partner who was insane. I said the only thing I could. "But I really don't think Ms. Brooks will let us do a science project on ESP."

Caroline let out a sigh, like she couldn't believe she had to work with me. "I'll go ask her, and then will you stop exuding all of this negative energy?"

Exuding? Negative energy?

"Sure," I said. "If Ms. Brooks says we can do a psychic science fair project, we'll do one."

Caroline pushed herself up from her chair, picked up her books and magazine, and flounced up to Ms. Brooks's desk. She handed Ms. Brooks the magazine, then spoke while waving a hand in my direction.

Ms. Brooks sighed, looked down at the books and magazine, flipped through a couple of pages, sighed again, said something I couldn't hear, and handed Caroline the magazine back.

Caroline returned to my desk with a triumphant smile. "She said we could do it."

"Are you kidding me?" For a woman who'd killed countless frogs over the years, I expected her to have a little more backbone.

"I think it was the issue of *Discover* that convinced her. It is a scientific magazine, after all."

"She said *yes*?"

Caroline opened her notebook and smoothed down the paper. "You know, Cami, you really need to work on your negative energy problem."

Yeah, well, I'd take that up right after I fixed all of my other problems.

Josie

I play basketball like it's a game. I play to have fun. Cami plays basketball like it's war. She plays to annihilate everyone else. She tries to psyche you out by staring in your eyes and murmuring, "You can't stop me. I am the ball."

As soon as we walked into the gym after school for practice, Cami was all determination and training. She actually ran hard for our first two warm-up laps. I struggled to keep up with her, then threatened to trip her if she didn't slow down. Coach Melbourne had created a monster with her stupid Rebecca Lobo reward.

I couldn't tell Cami about biology during the first two laps, because Ashley Holt and one of her lackeys, Erica Green, were right in front of us. I didn't want them to hear me talking about Ethan.

Even though Ashley and Ethan aren't going out at the moment, Ashley would probably still turn around and say something like, "You and Ethan together? When pigs fly."

And then Erica would add, "Pigs might fly someday. After all, they're already playing basketball with us."

Ashley is team captain, so you'd think she'd be nice to everyone, but mostly she just uses the position to boss people around. She especially doesn't like Cami and me because we're both better at basketball than she is, and we don't suck up to her like so many girls who just want the privilege of her friendship.

Besides, Ashley and Cami used to be friends back in sixth grade, then they had a fight and have been feuding ever since.

I think it physically pains Cami to have to throw the ball to Ashley during a game, but she does it anyway. Ashley is a good player, and Cami puts her feelings aside when it comes to winning. But outside of game time, the feud is back on.

When Cami and I slowed down during our third warm-up lap, Ashley and Erica pulled ahead of us, and I finally told Cami about biology and my science partner. ". . . So I asked Ethan, and he turned me down, but I don't know whether he wanted to be my partner but couldn't, or whether he was relieved he'd already agreed to be Brendan's partner because it gave him an excuse to say no to me. I don't know whether it was bad luck or rejection."

"We could ask my science fair partner. She has psychic powers."

"Really?"

Cami huffed in a way that had nothing to do with running. "No, not really. People don't have psychic powers, which is why my science project will be laughed out of the science fair. I bet you and Frederick win first prize."

"No, our rockets will probably explode on us. I mean, aren't they too dangerous for science projects? Don't they have rules about these things? Why couldn't I just study germs like Ethan?"

Cami laughed, and I knew what she was going to say before she said, "I'm sure there are enough girls studying germs like Ethan."

"Very funny. So how will I have my second conversation with him? I should probably start planning it now so I can think of something to say besides 'um' and 'so.'"

We finished the lap, and Cami put her hands on her hips,

breathing deeply. "How about the mall? Ethan was talking to Justin at his locker about going there tomorrow night. We'll show up, wander around until we run into them, and there's your second conversation."

"Okay." We walked over to the ball bin. Cami took two balls out and threw one to me. I let the ball bounce between my hands, feeling the strength of its spring. "I need to think of mall topics—"

"My parents won't be able to drive us though. They're going to Kevin's band concert."

"I'll ask my mom if she can drive."

Coach Melbourne blew her whistle, and we started our drills.

While I dribbled, I thought about Ethan, the mall, and about helping Cami with extra free-throw practice.

When was I going to find time to do my homework—especially writing three poems about myself? I tried to come up with something while I played.

What rhymed with basketball player? What rhymed with . . .

I couldn't think of anything else to say about myself.

These were either going to be three very short poems, or I was going to have to develop some interesting personality traits very quickly.

Words ran through my mind in the rhythm of the ball hitting the floor.

I-smack-play-smack-basketball.
Pivot, smack. I'm kinda tall.
Run, smack, jump, that's really all.

No wonder Ethan didn't know I was alive. I needed to be more . . . anything, everything. I needed to be popular, to be "in." I glanced over at Ashley. Even with her hair pulled back into a ponytail, even with a sheen of sweat across her face, she looked beautiful and confident. In class she had this way of tossing her hair off her shoulder that seemed so sophisticated. It was time for me to add some of that to my image. Tomorrow at the mall I'd be the very essence of sophistication.

Cami

I am the ball, I told myself over and over again during practice. I will be MVP.

When practice ended and everyone else headed toward the locker room, I tossed the ball to Josie. "Run another passing drill with me. How about a bounce pass going up and a chest pass coming back?"

Ashley sauntered by us, carrying her basketball under her arm. She'd taken her hair out of the ponytail, and it swung around her shoulders without even looking mussed. She nudged Erica and pointed at us. "Cosie and Jami are both wearing blue T-shirts. They're such clones, you can hardly tell them apart."

"Maybe you can't," I called after her, "but we don't expect much from you. You probably need name tags to tell your parents apart."

"And you don't," Ashley answered over her shoulder, "because you just remember your mother is the ugly one."

I dropped the basketball and lunged toward Ashley. Josie grabbed hold of my arm, pulling me back while Ashley and Erica hurried away from us. "Are you crazy?" Josie asked. "Do you want to get suspended from playing?"

"It'll be worth it."

"Not if she's the one who plays ball with Rebecca."

I tugged my arm away from Josie, but by then Ashley and Erica were halfway across the gym and heading quickly to the locker room.

Josie picked up our basketball and held it loosely against her hip. "I don't know why you let her get to you. I mean, it's not like your mother is really ugly."

I put my hands on my hips. "I don't know why you *don't* let her get to you. I mean, what would you do if she had called your mother ugly?"

"I would have said something like—" Josie shrugged. "'Judging by your looks, she's obviously not as ugly as your mom.'" She bounced the ball twice. "Ashley is just trying to psyche you out so you won't play well."

Ashley disappeared into the locker room, but I still stared after her. "She's rude and obnoxious, and if I'm not high scorer, and Ashley is, I want you to forget about our deal and do everything you can to beat her."

Josie laughed and dribbled the ball from hand to hand. "Come on, let's run some passing drills before they kick us out of the gym."

We ran back and forth across the court twice, and I tried to be the ball, instead of being a wad of anger, but it was hard. I kept reliving the conversation with Ashley, wishing I

had come up with Josie's retort, and wondering why she did-
n't say it to Ashley for me. ——

After the passing drill, we both took a few free throws.
Josie's went in, while mine ricocheted off the rim and sailed
across the gym with more force than I thought I'd put in them.
She was obviously not brooding about the Ashley incident, but
then Josie didn't know the whole truth about Ashley.

Ashley and I had become friends in the third grade, when
we were the only girls on our parks and rec basketball team.
We played together every recess, pretending we were pros.

Then in sixth grade, Ashley decided she wanted to be
popular, and Josie and I were holding her down. Especially
Josie. Back then I had glasses and braces, and Josie never
combed her hair or worried about wearing designer clothes,
stylish clothes, or even clean clothes.

I admit we were geeks, but after all, it was sixth grade, and
who really cared?

One day during a basketball game Ashley told me, "I think
you'd have more friends if you stopped hanging around Josie."

"I don't want to stop hanging around her," I said. "She's
nice."

Ashley just shrugged. "Well, I don't want to hang around
with her anymore. So you'll have to choose who's your best
friend."

The next day at recess I taught Josie how to play basketball. I hoped Ashley would join us, but she didn't. She hardly
talked to either of us after that, unless it was to make fun of us.

Josie and I have both improved since then. I now have
straight teeth and contacts. Josie combs her hair and wears—

well, she still wears jeans and T-shirts most of the time, but they're clean. And Ashley is still a snob.

On the car ride home, after I made a list of my homework assignments, I made a list of the reasons Josie and I are not clones.

1. Josie's hair is long brown, and mine is shoulder-length blond. If Ashley and Erica can't tell the difference between these hairstyles, they are more clueless than I thought.

2. Josie is two inches taller than me, which is just one of those unfairnesses of life, since I like basketball more, so therefore I should be taller.

3. Josie knows everything about Ethan, and I—well, I know everything about Ethan too, but that's mostly because she's told me. She has his locker combination, his phone number, and his address memorized. I only have his locker combination memorized—and that's because his locker is next to mine. I mean, how could I help but notice his combination?

4. Her room looks like a garbage truck capsized somewhere in the middle of it; mine is clean.

5. She laughs a lot, sometimes for no rational reason, like when she misses a basketball shot.

6. She thinks I'm cynical just because I don't believe everything everyone tells me. I'm not cynical. I'm just realistic about life.

Four

Josie

On the way home from practice Cami made a list of reasons why she and I are different. I know that's what she wrote because she wouldn't let me see it, and because she got all upset when Ashley called us clones and afterward kept saying things like, "We're different in a ton of ways. No one would really get us confused for one another."

We are different, but not in a ton of ways. We're so alike I can switch topics mid-conversation, and Cami still knows what I'm talking about. Sometimes we finish sentences for each other. I can see a shirt in a store and know whether Cami will like it or not. But there are differences. Cami is compulsively organized. She has color-coded her closet. The only thing that's ever on her floor is carpet, and the top of her dresser is dusted and polished. I don't worry about dusting my dresser, because the top of my dresser isn't visible. It's covered with books, pictures, pencils, makeup, dishes, and whatever I left in the family room that my mom threw on my bed while she was cleaning, and I then put on my dresser when I went to sleep.

Cami is also more intense. She fights for things harder and holds grudges longer. She can tell you who didn't come to her birthday party in first grade, and why. I can only tell you I was in first grade and probably had a birthday party at that time.

Oh, and I'm beginning to wonder if this thing she has for making lists is healthy. I mean, really, who spends the time to make a list of how they're different from their best friend? I've seen her daily to-do lists, and number one and number two are always: Get dressed and Eat breakfast. Does she actually need to be reminded to do those things? If she didn't have them on her list, would she come to school naked and hungry?

I don't make lists. If I remember something I need to do, I do it; and if I don't remember it, it probably wasn't that important.

Asking my mother to drive us to the mall was not something I needed to put on a list. Going to the mall was important. The cool kids hung out there. I had never been a mall wanderer before, because the mall is way more expensive than the places I buy clothes. I generally shop in stores that end with the word *mart, outlet,* or *thrift.* Besides, whenever I ask to go to the mall, my mother comes and generally brings my younger sisters and my five-year-old brother along. This is a totally uncool thing to do.

On TV, teenagers always have perfect hair and perfect clothes, and they never say stupid stuff. Apparently to be cool I need a makeup artist, a wardrobe assistant, and a personal writer to slip me dialogue before I open my mouth.

Being "in" is harder than it looks.

While Mom made dinner that night, I went into the kitchen to talk to her. I had learned this was not the best time to talk to my mother—in fact, this was not the best time to be in the same room with her, because if you happened to be around, you automatically were enlisted to help.

Still, I walked up to her. "Mom, can you take Cami and me to the mall tomorrow night?"

She shoved a block of cheese into the food processor and turned it on. "Isn't it your turn to sweep the floor?"

"Yeah. Sure." I went to the side of the refrigerator where we kept our broom and took it out. "Cami's parents can't take us, because they're going to her brother's band concert. Besides, they took us the last time, so can you do it tomorrow?"

"Don't forget the corners. Things are beginning to accumulate back there."

"You wouldn't have to stay the whole time. You could just drop us off and then pick us up."

She turned off the processor. "You're too young to walk around the mall by yourself."

"I'm in high school now." I held out my hands as though she ought to see all of the maturity flowing off my body. "None of the other freshmen have parents who follow them around."

She sprinkled the cheese over a pan of chicken enchiladas.

"Really, Mom, it's the mall, not some drug-infested back alleyway. I'll be fine." I didn't tell her Cami's parents routinely dropped us off places by ourselves. I was afraid she'd start vetoing my outings if she knew.

Mom put the pan into the oven. "It's a fifteen-minute drive. It would take me half an hour to drop you off and come home again. Then another thirty minutes to come pick you up and bring you back home. And of course I'll have to drag all the kids along."

"Why can't they stay with Dad?"

"Dad's working late for a couple of nights. He's got a quarterly report to finish."

"Well, can't you just—" I didn't finish the question. I knew Mom wouldn't leave my sisters and brother alone to drive me somewhere.

Kristen was eleven, Sadie was nine—and both reasonably intelligent beings—but heaven forbid Mom leave them alone in the house for half an hour with Jack. It was like Mom was afraid the roof might spontaneously combust and no one would have a clue to call 911.

Mom's view of the conversation my siblings would have while the house was burning:

KRISTEN: So, I notice there are flames leaping from the ceiling. Do you suppose that's a bad thing?

SADIE: I'm not sure. Let's watch it for a while and see if it gets worse.

KRISTEN: While we're watching, let's get the marshmallows out and make s'mores.

SADIE: Well, we're not supposed to get into treats while Mom is gone, but I won't tell if you won't.

JACK: We're making s'mores? Can I have powdered sugar on mine?

I mean, I've read the entire *Little House on the Prairie* series, and back then eleven-year-olds drove teams of horses over rugged terrain past wild bears just to go into town, and my mom is afraid to leave her children alone in the living room.

I tried to point this out to her gently.

"Mom, you're way too overprotective."

Mom set the buzzer on the oven. "Jack is only five years old."

I held my hands up in the air, pleading my case. "Kristen and Sadie are old enough to babysit him for a half an hour while you take me to the mall."

She put the cheese bowl in the dishwasher and shut it with a click. "Kristen and Sadie can't remember to feed the dog, let alone watch after their little brother. Don't forget to sweep under the counters. Jack spilled Cheerios over there."

I walked over to the edge of the counter, running the broom against the baseboard. "So are you going to take us? I need to tell Cami."

"I'll take you, but as long as I'm driving all the way out there, I might as well stay and do some shopping. The fall stuff is on clearance, and I can pick up some things for next year."

Mom is a bargain shopper. She says if you can't get something at least 50 percent off, it isn't worth owning. She doesn't even look at the normal racks in a store. My entire wardrobe has come from the clearance sales that stores have before they send the remainder of a clothing line to the fashion graveyard.

It didn't used to bother me, but lately I've wondered if

everyone knows when they look at me—like maybe the reason I'm not one of the "in" kids is that my clothes are always a year behind the trend.

Mom took a bag of peas from the freezer, dumped them into a bowl, and put them in the microwave. "I hear Sears has a few swimsuits left on the seventy-five-percent-off rack. You need a new swimsuit, don't you?"

Unfortunately I didn't. I kept hoping that—just like all those videos they made us watch in health class—my body would magically metamorphose into a curvy womanlike structure, but it didn't. I look exactly like I did in the seventh grade, only taller. I'm five foot eight and a half and can wear a lot of Kristen's clothes. I might never need a new swimsuit, but I didn't tell my mother this. I just shrugged and turned the conversation back to the mall.

"You're not actually going to be shopping with us, right? You'll let Cami and me go by ourselves, and then we'll meet you somewhere to go home, right?"

"You don't want to be seen at the mall with your mother?"

"Right."

Mom took a dishcloth, dampened it under the faucet, and wrung it out. "Having a mother isn't like having a disease, you know. Everyone you see at the mall has a mother."

But not with them, holding up swimsuits while calling out, Look, Josie, it's only five dollars. I think we could make it fit if we took in the top a few inches.

At this point Kristen walked into the kitchen. "You're going to the mall? Can I come?"

Mom ran the dishcloth over the counter. "We're all going, but Josie wants to pretend she's an orphan."

"An orphan with no brothers or sisters," I added.

"Can I get some new shirts?" Kristen asked. "I don't have anything to wear."

Mom paused in her counter wiping, her head cocked at Kristen. "You're in the sixth grade now. I think it's time we get you a couple of training bras."

"Bras?" Kristen spit out the word like Mom had just suggested she buy a pair of cobras. "I don't want to wear a bra."

"A training bra," Mom said. "It's not a big deal."

Jack wandered into the kitchen, carrying two plastic dinosaurs. "What's a training bra?"

"Never mind," Mom said.

"How is Kristen going to train it?" he asked.

"Go wash your hands," Mom said. "It's almost time for dinner."

Jack's shoulders slumped, and he shuffled out of the kitchen. "Nobody ever tells me anything."

Kristen followed him, her arms folded. Over her shoulder she mouthed the words, "I'm not bra shopping with him."

"I'm not bra shopping with anybody," I said. "I'm an orphan."

Cami

Sometimes my brother turns up his radio too loud, but besides that, my house is pretty calm and quiet.

Things are different at the Caraway house. It's constant motion. Constant noise. Someone is always talking, walking by you, crawling over you, or asking if you've seen their homework.

Sometimes, when Josie and her sisters all sit around laughing about something, I feel cheated I never had a sister. Other times, all the commotion makes my head pound.

The car ride to the mall was commotion. Kristen was sulking, Sadie was complaining because she didn't want to go to the mall ("Why do I have to go? I don't need a bra. The mall is just boring. Boooring. Boriiing."), and Jack kept leaning over the back of his seat to tell me about dog tricks.

"You can train a dog to fetch," he said.

"That's nice."

"You can train them to sit, too."

"Great."

Every time Jack said the word *train*, Josie broke out laughing, and Kristen folded her arms tighter and stared out the window.

"You can train them to play dead, too," he said.

"Yes, I'm sure you can."

Jack put his chin on the seat. "Our hamster never played dead. He was just dead. And I don't think that counts as a trick."

Kristen pulled Jack off the back of the seat, which made him yell, "Hey!" Only he didn't yell it like a one syllable word. He yelled it like it was one of the longer words in the English language. "H-e-e-e-e-e-e-e-e-e-e-e-ey."

"Be quiet," she hissed.

"I don't have to," he said.

"Yes, you do," she said.

They argued about this point for the rest of the trip. When we got to the mall, there was more fighting.

"I'm not shopping with Jack along," Kristen said.

He stuck his tongue out at her.

Josie's mom looked at us, but Josie held her hands up. "I'm an orphan, remember?"

"You can take him just until I'm finished shopping with Kristen. It won't take long."

Kristen folded her arms and grunted. "Thanks a lot."

Mrs. Caraway looked around the store as though she was trying to locate one of the departments. "How about we meet back here in half an hour, and I'll take Jack with me then." She took Jack's hand and gave it to Josie. "Actually, let's say thirty-five minutes, in case we run into a line at the cashier."

She walked a few paces away, then turned and called out, "Make that forty-five minutes. Since I'm here, I might as well buy a bra for myself. My old ones are getting ratty."

"Mother!" Kristen hissed. "Would you please not talk about your bras in the middle of Sears."

Mrs. Caraway just clicked her tongue. "Honestly, Kristen, do you think we're the only ones who've ever bought bras? I bet every woman you see here is wearing a bra."

Kristen rolled her eyes and stomped off toward the lingerie department, arms still folded tightly.

Sadie followed after her, giggling. "You don't need to be in such a hurry, Kristen." More giggling. "Keep your shirt on."

Josie sighed, and pulled Jack toward the mall entrance. "I'm supposed to be an orphan."

"Where are we going?" Jack asked. "Can we go to the pet store?"

As we walked past the makeup department, the mall hallway came into view. "Not now," Josie said. "We're going . . . um . . . where do you want to go for forty-five minutes, Cami?"

With a five-year-old boy in tow? Nowhere.

I shrugged. "Let's just walk around and look at stuff. It's not like we can try things on while we've got Jack with us anyway."

Josie nodded, and we sauntered out into the mall. Jack jabbered on about the pet store, asking if we thought they had hamsters and whether or not his mom would let him have a new one. He knew where the pet store was, and since we were walking in that general direction, he must have thought we were going there.

Josie kept hold of his hand, but didn't answer him. Her gaze darted down the hall and into the stores. I knew she was looking for Ethan.

We walked down the mall, every once in a while stopping in front of a window to look at clothes.

"How do you think I should change my image?" Josie asked me after peering at a snug-fitting red shirt on a mannequin. "Do I need to be more sophisticated, or more playful, or more feminine? What do you think I need more of?"

"Common sense. A shirt isn't going to change your personality."

"If it's the right shirt, it might."

"Your personality is fine. Although, now that you mention it, you could try to be on time more. You're always running late."

Josie cocked her head. "You think that bothers Ethan?"

"No. It bothers me though."

She glared at me, turned away from the window, and continued walking down the mall. We weaved around other shoppers while we looked for the guys.

"You also procrastinate about doing your homework, and you laugh when you shouldn't," I said.

"What are you talking about? I don't laugh when I shouldn't."

"Yes, you do. Remember when Kevin first got his license and was driving us to the football game? The car stalled in the middle of the intersection, cars were honking at us, and Kevin twisted the key so hard it made that horrible grinding sound. I thought we were going to die, and you sat there laughing."

She held out a hand as though explaining. "That's why it was funny."

"You're hopeless. Which I suppose counts as a personality defect. Do you think you could buy a shirt to fix that?" I knew I was being mean, but somehow I couldn't help it. Ethan was here somewhere, and when we found him, Josie would go up and flirt with him. He'd gaze into her eyes, flirt back, and I'd have to stand there and watch them fall in love. Then Josie would have him, just like she got everything she wanted—and despite our deal, Coach Melbourne would probably still choose her to play with Rebecca.

Josie swung Jack's hand as we walked and smiled at me, even though I'd just told her she was hopeless. "All right, so what I need is a hopeful shirt."

What was wrong with me? Josie was my best friend. There were hundreds of guys at our school. Why had I chosen to like the guy my best friend liked? I needed to forget about Ethan for as long as Josie liked him.

"You're not hopeless," I told her. "Your personality is fine, and you don't need to change yourself. Just show him the smart, funny girl you are. Say something clever and witty to him."

I was a good friend.

I was loyal.

I was not going to flirt with the guy Josie liked.

Besides, I didn't know if Ethan and Justin had actually come. I was stressing out over nothing. We probably wouldn't run into them at all.

"There he is." Josie pointed down the hallway. "Over there."

I had to quell the urge to push her out of the way to get a better look.

He had just come up the escalator with Justin and was walking over to the Foot Locker.

Josie took a step toward him, then immediately turned around and took two steps in the opposite direction.

"Where are you going?" I called.

"I changed my mind," she said. "I don't want to talk to him."

If she was always too afraid to talk to him, and I wasn't . . . and I saw him every day at English and at my locker . . .

I followed her, grabbing on to her elbow. "You can't chicken out now. This is why you came to the mall and dragged the rest of us with you. Your poor sister is somewhere in Sears flipping through training bras and praying no one she knows strolls by, just so you could talk to this guy. You can't leave now."

Jack suddenly noticed we had turned away from the pet store and tried to pull away from Josie. "He-e-e-e-e-e-e-ey! I want to see the animals."

Josie turned around, facing the pet store so Jack would stop whining. "Jack, we're deciding where to go next."

"B-u-u-u-u-u-t—"

"We won't take you at all if you aren't good," Josie said.

He stopped whining, but furrowed his eyebrows and stuck out his bottom lip in a frown.

She whispered to me, "I can't walk up to him with my little brother. That's totally uncool."

"No, it's not. It's cute. And it shows you're responsible. Your mother trusts you to watch him."

Josie looked back down the mall, then at Jack, and didn't move.

I took Jack's hand. "I'll pretend he's my little brother, okay?" I bent down toward Jack. "If you'll be my brother, I'll take you to the pet store, all right?"

Josie shook her head. "It won't work. I mean, if Ethan

ever came to my house or something, he'd wonder why your little brother is living with me." She glanced back down the mall to where Justin and Ethan stood looking at things in Foot Locker's window. "We'll find them again after we drop Jack off with my mom." She pulled Jack toward one of the store entrances. "Right now we'll visit"—she looked up at the sign— "the Kitchen Nook, and keep an eye on the guys until it's time to go back to Sears."

"I don't want to go in this store," Jack said.

"Yes, you do. They have toys in this store. Here—" She took a red plastic chicken from the shelf. "Look at this egg timer."

Great. I was going to spend my evening hiding among kitchen utensils with a five-year-old boy.

I stepped into the store and sighed. "I just want to know one thing. How many crushes do you think you'll have from now until we graduate from high school? I want to know how many stalker skills I need to develop."

Josie walked farther down the aisle but kept her gaze on the mall hallway. "Just wait. Just wait until you like a guy, and then we'll see how you act."

Five

Josie

Cami says I'm overly dramatic. I don't think so. I just think my life has an abundance of tragedy.

Like the moment in the Kitchen Nook when Jack asked the woman standing next to us if she was wearing a bra.

After I stopped gasping and could speak, I told the woman, "I'm *so* sorry." Then I pulled Jack farther down the aisle, and started giggling—which goes to show you Cami is right about me laughing when I'm not supposed to.

"That is not a question you ask strangers," I told him.

He pulled his arm away from me. "But Mom said everyone wears a bra."

I tried to grab his arm again, but he turned away from me and bumped into a shelf. A pig-shaped cookie jar tumbled to the ground and broke into two pieces. That was another tragedy because I then had to pay $18.99 for something that now looked like a decapitated pig head.

The cookie jar squealed when you opened the lid. Of course *that* part didn't break. Jack opened and closed it two hundred times while I stood in line at the cash register to pay for it.

"Nineteen dollars for a cookie jar," I told Cami after we'd walked away from the salesclerk. "That is so overpriced. Now I won't have enough money to buy a shirt."

Jack flipped open the lid for the two-hundred-and-first time. *Squeeeal!*

I was ready to break the thing some more.

"It could have been worse," Cami said. "He could have broken one of those two-hundred-dollar bread makers."

I peered down the walkway. There was no sign of Ethan and Justin. They'd probably gone home.

Another tragedy.

"Can we go to the pet store now?" Jack asked.

I shoved the receipt in my purse and continued to look down through the mall, as though Ethan and Justin would appear again. They could have gone anywhere while we'd been in line paying for the cookie jar. They could have walked right past us.

Apparently Cami needed to brush up on her stalking skills quickly if she was going to help me through my school career of crushes.

Jack tugged at my hand, and I let out a sigh. "All right. We'll go to the pet store, but on one condition. You've got to stop squealing that pig."

He nodded solemnly, then went down the walkway with the broken cookie jar wrapped in his arms.

I didn't hold his hand anymore because both of his hands were on the cookie jar, but I kept one eye on him. Jack had a tendency to dart off; and if I didn't pay attention, I would be brotherless before I could say, "Mom will kill me."

I was keeping such a good eye on Jack, I didn't see Ethan until I ran into him.

I mean, I didn't actually run into him. I just practically ran into him. He had to sidestep me, and so he dropped the shopping bag he was carrying. A pair of tennis shoes tumbled out onto the floor.

"Oh. Sorry," I said, remembering Cami's advice to say something clever and witty to him.

"That's okay." He bent down and picked up one shoe while I picked up the other.

Clever and witty. Clever and witty.

I handed the shoe back to him. "So you bought new shoes. I like them."

He put the shoe back in the bag. "These are the old ones. I'm wearing the new ones."

"Right. That's what I meant. I like the ones you're wearing." I looked at his feet for the first time.

He wore black tennis shoes. I nodded at them as though admiring his laces. "Very nice."

"Are you here shoe shopping?" he asked.

"No, we're just hanging out. Looking at stuff . . ." I noticed he was staring at Jack's cookie jar. "Breaking things," I added.

Jack, apparently bored that we'd stopped walking again, opened the cookie jar. It let out a squeal.

Justin raised an eyebrow. "I can see why you broke it."

Jack clutched the pig head to his chest, then walked

toward the railing that overlooked the ground floor. "The pet store is downstairs," he yelled to us, and took a few steps toward the escalator.

Cami called, "Come back here." Then in a lower voice she said to Ethan, "Jack wants to see the animals. He's, um, my little brother."

I smiled stiffly at Ethan and Justin. "He visits my house with Cami a lot." I turned to check on Jack and saw him sticking the pig head through the railing bars.

And suddenly I could see the headlines of tomorrow's newspaper:

MALL SHOPPER KILLED BY FALLING PIG HEAD.
OLDER SISTER CHARGED WITH NEGLIGENCE

"Jack, come here right now and give me that cookie jar!" I yelled.

He didn't move. "I won't drop it."

I snapped my fingers at him and raised my voice louder. "If you want to live to see six candles on your next birthday cake, you'll come here this second and give me that pig!"

Ethan and Justin exchanged a look—probably wondering why I was shouting at Cami's little brother—but what else could I do when Jack wasn't listening to me?

Jack trotted back to us and with an exaggerated sigh handed me the cookie jar.

"Thanks, Jack," Cami said sweetly. She apparently was a nice sister who didn't yell at her little brother after he nearly killed shoppers.

Jack looked back toward the banister and the bottom floor of the mall. "I think they have hamsters down there. I want to get one and train it."

Ethan grinned. "You can't train a hamster."

"Uh-huh," Jack said. "You can train anything. Even a bra."

I laughed because I could think of nothing else to do, except for bolting away from everyone, which in the long run would have been even more awkward than standing there laughing.

"Oh, really?" Justin said. "What do you train them to do?"

Jack shrugged. "I don't know. My sister won't tell me, but she's getting a training bra."

Both Justin and Ethan turned and looked at Cami. She held up one hand and shook her head. "He's not really my brother."

"I think it has something to do with rats," Jack said. "Because Mom said her bra was ratty."

"Not my bra," Cami said, "Jack's mother's bra. She said *her* bra was ratty."

Justin nodded, eyebrows raised. Ethan smirked.

"I'm absolutely no relation to this child," Cami said. "He's Josie's brother."

Ethan and Justin simultaneously turned and looked at me.

I clutched the pig head harder. "No, he's not." Not as long as he was telling the guy I liked that his sister had a ratty training bra. I sent a stiff smile to Cami. "Cami always tries to disown him when he misbehaves."

I turned to give Jack a neighborly I'm-so-glad-I'm-not-your-sister-now pat on the head, but he wasn't there. My gaze swung from one side of shops to the other, trying to find him. "Where did he—" I asked, then located him just as he went down the escalator.

"Jack!" I called.

He didn't answer.

I rushed over to the escalator, my purse flapping against my side, and the pig head tucked under one arm. Not only had Jack gone down the escalator, but he'd gone down the up escalator.

For a moment I waited at the top to see if the upward motion of the stairs would be faster than his determination to get down them. If he wasn't quick enough, the stairs would just carry him back up to me, where I would grab him and immediately drag him back to my mother.

He was making progress; his little legs jiggled on the stairs as he wove around a group of teenagers coming up. In a few more moments he'd be down on the ground floor, where I might lose him for good.

Which meant I had to go after him.

I took a breath and plunged down the stairs. The pig head was still tucked under my arm like a football, and I wished I had given it to Cami before I'd dashed after Jack. I held on to it tightly so as not to drop the thing as I attempted to outrace my brother. It felt as though I was hardly moving, like one of those dreams where you run but don't go anywhere. I was hurrying as quickly as I could and making slow progress. The people coming up, however, were traveling fast. I could see their disapproving faces as I stepped down past them.

"Hey, this is the up escalator," one guy told me.

Oh, really? And here I thought someone had installed Stairmaster exercise equipment in the middle of the mall.

I was almost to Jack. I tried to move around a woman who was trying to move around me at the same time. Caught off balance, I grabbed hold of the handrailing for support.

Which might have helped if I were going the same direction as the handrailing.

Instead, the rising motion of the railing nearly jerked my arm out of my socket. I was pulled backward, and as I struggled to regain my balance, I lost my footing and stumbled forward.

From there, my trip down the escalator was a blur of people gasping and trying not to step on me. I heard the pig head squealing somewhere ahead of me.

Thunk. Squeal. Thunk. Squeal. Thunk. Squeal. Crash.

I didn't see its ultimate demise. My face was planted downward, so all I could see were the metal slats that made up the stairs.

As I lay there spread out on the escalator like some furless bear rug, the stairs took me back up to the second floor. Once I reached the top, I twisted around, trying to peel myself away from the escalator, while the people behind me kept stepping backward down the stairs so they didn't run into me.

Suddenly I saw Justin's face hovering over me, and then he half yanked, half pulled me away from the stairs. "Are you all right?"

I stumbled to my feet, trying to shake off the pain. I probably had slat imprints on my face. "Where's Jack?"

"Cami went around to the down escalator to get him. She nabbed him about the time you were coming back up."

"Great." I took a few small steps to see if I could still walk. I could. Nothing appeared to be broken. I mean, I didn't see any bones sticking out of my skin or anything.

Ethan shook his head at me, trying not to laugh. "Man, Josie, I should start carrying a camcorder when I'm around you. The last five minutes could have won me prize money on *America's Funniest Home Videos*."

I rubbed my hands together to relieve the stinging. "Anything to bring a little humor into your life, Ethan."

"Are you all right?" Justin asked again.

Oh, sure. This was the second time I'd fallen on my face in front of Ethan, and the only saving grace was that it had driven all thoughts of bras from his mind.

"I will be in a minute," I said.

Ethan chuckled some more, which made me wonder if my hair was sticking up or something. I ran a hand over it just in case.

"You shouldn't have followed Jack down the escalator," Justin said. "You should have just let his sister get him."

It was about that time that Jack and Cami stepped off the up escalator.

"But I want to get a new hamster!" Jack insisted.

"And instead you got a broken cookie jar that squeals. Be happy."

"I don't think it's squealing anymore." Justin nodded toward the escalator, where little pink ceramic fragments were spinning on the grate with every stair that came up.

"That's my pig?" Jack wailed. "You broke my pig?"

I took Jack's hand. "We'd better go, Cami."

"He's really not my brother," Cami said.

Jack's face crumpled. His eyes blinked at the pig shards. "You *broke* my pig?"

I pulled Jack away from Ethan and Justin without saying good-bye to them. I just wanted to get away, and fast. When I was sure we were out of earshot, I said, "That was definitely the most uncool I've ever been."

"It could have been worse," Cami said.

I held on to Jack's hand tightly, pulling him beside me. "Right. My little brother has become a bra commentator. I spent all my money on ceramic pig debris, and I fell down an escalator in front of dozens of mall shoppers and the guy I like. From here on out he will remember me only as that-strange-girl-who-spends-most-of-her-time-facedown-on-the-ground. It could not have been worse."

Cami pursed her lips together. "You're right," she said, then giggled all the way back to Sears. Which just goes to prove she's no better about laughing at the wrong times than I am.

Cami

On the car trip home, Jack whined and complained about his broken pig until Josie promised to give him one of her Beanie Babies when they got back home. Then Josie whined and complained about why she couldn't go to the mall—just once—as an only child. "I'll never be 'in,' " she said sullenly. "Unless you count '*in*sane,' which is what I must have been to agree to go to the mall with my family."

I didn't complain about the event, even though it was just as humiliating for me as it was for Josie. I mean, anyone can trip; it takes someone truly unlucky to be labeled as the girl with the ratty training bra.

I knew I would hear about that from now until graduation.

Besides, Josie would probably stop liking Ethan next week and could avoid him for the rest of her life. I'd be stuck seeing him at my locker all year.

On Friday morning, sure enough, as I was getting math stuff out of my locker, Ethan came by. He twirled the combination of his locker, then looked over at me and chuckled.

"Shut up," I told him.

"I can't help it. I'm imagining trained rats wearing little bras."

I glared at him over the top of my locker. "Jack is five years old. He gets a lot of things wrong. Until recently he thought Ronald McDonald personally made his Happy Meals."

Ethan pulled a notebook from his locker, then waved a pencil at me. "I want to have another conversation with Jack. I bet for a Snickers bar he'd spill all of your secrets."

"I'm sure he'd try, but he really is Josie's brother, not mine."

Ethan tilted his head at me. "Then why did you say he was yours?"

"You wouldn't understand."

He leaned around with a grin. "Sure I would. I'm very understanding. It's one of my better qualities."

Ashley walked by us from her locker a few feet down. She smiled pointedly at Ethan. "He knows all about his better qualities because there are so few to keep track of."

Ethan shut his locker with a thud. "Good to see you too, Ash."

"If you ever want to know about his other qualities," she told me, "I'd be happy to fill you in."

Ethan's eyes narrowed. "And we could talk about your other qualities, but there isn't enough time in one day to cover them all."

Ashley tossed her hair off her shoulder and walked forward as though she'd never seen either of us.

Ethan watched her go. His eyes were still narrow, and for a moment I thought he'd completely forgotten about me. Then he leaned up against his locker and smiled at me again. "Where were we?"

"I'm not sure, but there were no rats involved."

He laughed and ran a hand through his hair. His eyes twinkled.

I reminded myself that I was Josie's good friend, and loyal, and something else. I suddenly couldn't remember what, with Ethan smiling at me.

"So do you really have a brother?" Ethan asked.

"Yep."

"Would he spill all your secrets for a Snickers bar?"

"Maybe."

"Can I have your phone number so I can talk to him?"

It actually took me several seconds to process his question. Ethan had just asked me for my phone number. Ethan. Gorgeous, available Ethan.

And then, although I hadn't planned to, although I wasn't even done thinking about the implications of this question, my lips said my phone number.

He wrote it down on his notebook. "What's his name?"

"Who?"

"Your brother—what's his name?"

"Kevin."

"Great. Maybe I'll give Kevin a call tonight."

He walked away. I held my books against my chest, rooted to the spot, and watched him disappear into the throng of students in the hallway.

He was going to call me. What would he say? What would I say?

If I was a good friend, I ought to talk about Josie, tell him what a great person she was. And after all, maybe that was the real reason he wanted to talk to me. Maybe he wanted me to act as a go-between for Josie and him.

I didn't need to feel guilty about him asking for my phone number.

But as I thought of his smile, I felt guilty anyway.

Six

Josie

During English class I tried to toss my hair from my shoulder in the same sophisticated way Ashley did. But I don't know whether I looked sophisticated or as though I had neck spasms.

Sophistication obviously took practice.

While I was shooting warm-ups at basketball practice Frederick walked into the gym, a bulging backpack slung over his shoulders.

From beside me Erica shot her ball into the net. "What's he doing in here?"

Ashley stopped dribbling and stared at him. "He's probably here to critique our technique and tell us algorithms that would increase our accuracy."

I aimed and threw. My ball arched toward the basket, but fell short. "He's my science fair partner. He probably came in to talk to me."

"Oh." Ashley blew me a kiss. "Frederick and Josie. How romantic. We'll be sure to let everyone know you're a couple."

"Yeah, and I'd let everyone know you're a couple of idiots," I said as I walked up court, "but most people already know."

I picked up my ball and went over to the sidelines, where Frederick was waiting for me.

He didn't say hi or make small talk. As soon as I got within earshot, he told me, "I've attached lead tape to the nose and fins of the rockets. We need to measure their center of gravity and weigh them before they're launched. When are you through in here?"

"Four fifteen."

"I've got the rockets with me. Mr. Parkinson said we could use the scales in the biology room. I'll be waiting for you there."

After practice I'm hot, sweaty, and starving. Nobody from the team showers in the locker because the locker-room towels are tiny, the water takes forever to get hot, and given the choice, we'd all rather go home and use our own bathrooms than stand around naked in front of each other. The last thing I wanted to do after practice was hang out with Frederick in the biology room. "You've already started our project—two days after Mrs. Parkinson gave us the assignment?"

"Yes," he said, like it was a ridiculous question.

"Couldn't we wait to measure them sometime when I haven't been running sprints all afternoon?"

He grunted. "You're telling me you're too exhausted from basketball practice to weigh a rocket?"

I pushed the strands of hair that had escaped my ponytail back behind one ear. "Fine, have it your way. I'll meet you in the biology room after practice."

"Fine." He walked away muttering something about jock-ettes, and I went back to practice, trying to sweat less so my T-shirt wouldn't be sticking to my body when I saw him next.

Which didn't work.

After practice I went out to the parking lot and explained the situation to my mom, who'd come to give Cami and me a ride home. Our parents took turns giving us rides from practice, since we lived in the same neighborhood.

"How long will you be?" Mom asked.

"I don't know. I'll call you."

She sighed, like it was a burden to drive the five minutes to the school to pick me up again, which it probably was, considering she dragged Jack with her everywhere. He was bouncing up and down in the backseat.

"I wish you'd told me about this beforehand," she said.

"I didn't know about it beforehand. My project is on rockets, not ESP. Camilla should have been the one to predict it for you."

Cami rolled her eyes at me and climbed into my car.

I watched them pull out of the parking lot, then walked back into the school and went to the biology room. Frederick had the rockets set up by the table and was sitting at one of the desks, reading a science fiction novel. Which figured. Not only did he know all about rockets, he was probably devising space-travel techniques in his spare time.

He put the book down when I came in. "Good, you're finally here." He stood and walked to the nearest rocket holding it up for me to see. "While we measure the rockets I'll explain the project to you. I've used lead tape on the nose and behind the fins to move the rocket's center of gravity. We'll also change two of the rockets' centers of pressure by cutting some of the fins off. Then we'll launch the rockets and record their trajectories and flight times, proving that to be stable, the rocket's center of gravity has to be forward of the center of pressure." He put the rocket back on the counter. "Why are you staring at me like that?"

"I'm waiting for you to start speaking English."

He held his hands up in frustration. "What didn't you understand? I thought you said you were smart."

"I am smart, Frederick, I'm just not fluent in rocket-ese."

He shook his head. "Great. Not only do I have to do the experiment, I have to teach you basic aerodynamic principles along the way. This is exactly why I wanted to work alone."

I put my hands on my hips. "And this is exactly why no one wanted to work with you. Can you even have a conversation without insulting everyone else? If you don't want to teach me aerodynamic principles, we can do a different project. I would have been happy with a nail polish project, remember?"

He picked up a rocket and placed it on the scale. "Nail polish. How did you even get into advanced biology?"

"I got A's in science last year."

He huffed and then wrote down a number in his notebook. "That's the problem with teachers. They give extra credit out for being pretty. You probably just smiled and said, 'I left my assignment at home.' And your teachers said, 'Don't worry about it, honey. I'll give you an A-plus anyway.'"

"For your information, I did all of the assignments and

never got—" I grinned and leaned against the counter. "You think I'm pretty?"

He huffed again and gave me a condescending stare. "And that's the problem with girls. All you care about is your looks." He took one rocket off the scale and replaced it with another. "Intelligence doesn't matter to anyone. I'm the smartest guy in our class, and everyone hates me for it."

"No, everyone hates you for being so obnoxious about it. Your being smart doesn't really bother anyone."

He wrote down the weight of the rocket, then placed another rocket on the scale. "The school doesn't give out letter jackets for getting straight As. Only the jocks get those. Smart people don't get cheerleaders or pep rallies. I bet Bill Gates got no respect in high school. Now he could buy all those athletic teams you want to be on. Think about that."

I didn't think about Bill Gates, but as Frederick lectured me about the center of gravity, the center of pressure, and the difference between the two, I did think about all of the reasons he was annoying. The fact that he was forcing me to listen to this stuff topped the list.

I just wanted to get this project over as soon as possible so I didn't have to spend more time with him.

Cami

When I got home, I was still thinking about practice. I estimated how long it would take for my free throws to noticeably improve and wondered if it would be impolite to ask

Rebecca a lot of questions about the WNBA, like—when they're not playing games, do they get together and do girl things like go shoe shopping, or do they do one another's hair? I forgot all about Ethan's phone call until I walked into the family room and saw Kevin stretched out on the couch with the phone pressed against his ear.

"No, I wouldn't say it's *that* bad."

I stood in front of him, waving one hand to get his attention. I mouthed, "I'm expecting a phone call."

He glanced at me, then looked away without responding. Into the phone he said, "Nothing I can think of right off-hand."

I put my backpack on the floor and went into the kitchen to find something to eat. Mom was warming up frozen lasagna in the microwave, but it wouldn't be done for another fifteen minutes. Mom hardly ever cooked. She usually came home from work so frazzled from her job as a junior high teacher that just unthawing something took all her energy.

I took a banana from the counter and peeled it while I kicked off my shoes and waited for Kevin to get off the phone.

"It's pretty clean as far as rooms go," Kevin said. "No frilly pink stuff, although she still keeps Mr. Bunny and Miss Kitty on her shelf."

I put my banana down. "Who are you talking to?" I called into the family room.

Kevin didn't answer me. "I'd say her first love was Fred from *Scooby-Doo.* She used to go up to the TV and kiss it when he was on."

I sprinted into the family room.

"Yeah, I'm sure Fred felt jilted when she started watching the Jackie Chan show. Jackie has better muscles. Chicks go for that."

I jumped on to the couch and grabbed the phone, wrestling it out of Kevin's hands while he laughed. Finally I took the phone and walked down the hallway to my room. "Who is this?"

"Hey, Cami, you sound out of breath," Ethan said. "Or is heavy breathing just the way you greet people on the phone?"

I made it to my room, shut the door, and leaned up against the wall. "Ethan, I can't believe you were actually talking to Kevin about me."

"And I can't believe you had a thing for Jackie Chan. The man is old enough to be your father."

"Yeah, well, I wasn't so picky about guys in the fourth grade."

"Are you pickier now?"

"Oh, sure. Now I never go for the guys who are cartoons. My motto is: If his wardrobe comes from a pencil, I will not be going out with him."

Ethan laughed. I liked the way it sounded over the phone. I could almost see him with his head tilted back and his bangs falling across his forehead. "I feel the same way. Sure all those Anime girls are nice, but the girls I date have to have a nose somewhere on their face. That's where I draw the line—even though the artist didn't."

"I have a nose," I said.

"I noticed that," he said. "And my clothes don't come from a pencil."

Ethan had not called to talk to me about Josie.

I sat down on my bed, smiling, and felt completely happy.

Josie

The phone rang. A moment later Sadie poked her head into my bedroom. In a singsong voice she said, "A boy is on the phone for you."

Sometimes I hate being the oldest.

I grabbed the phone away from her and pushed her out of my bedroom, then locked the door.

Please let it be Ethan. Please let it be Ethan and not some misguided salesman who thinks I'm thirty-five and is trying to sell me a time-share condo. "Hello?"

"Hello, Josie, this is Frederick. Can you get together Saturday morning at the football field to shoot off rockets?"

"Oh." I tried not to sound disappointed but probably failed. "Sure. I don't have anything else planned."

Which was unfortunately the story of my life.

We agreed on the time, and I hung up the phone. Then I sat down on my bed, pulled out my English notebook, and doodled flowers while I tried to think of a poem about myself. Twenty minutes later I e-mailed the results to Cami.

ODE TO A BAD SCIENCE PROJECT

There once was a pretty young jockette
who was forced to launch off a rocket,
but when it was loaded
the project exploded;
now her fingers are worn in a locket.

CamE: Great limerick. I'd write a poem entitled "Ode to My Science Partner," but I can't think of any words that rhyme with "delusional." Did I tell you she's considering "pet psychic" as one of her career choices?

JoC1: A pet psychic? I never knew people kept psychics as pets.

CamE: No, she doesn't want to be a pet, she wants to help them. Like if your pet is having some sort of problem, you take it in for a consultation, and she tells you all about the inner turmoil that's going on in your guinea pig's mind.

JoC1: Maybe you can make an appointment for your cat. There is obviously something wrong with a creature that willingly drinks from the toilet.

Cami

After I finished IMing Josie, my conscience kicked into overdrive. I thought about Josie's other two poems for English. She would probably write about how she had a crush on "this guy." While I had just talked to "this guy" on the phone, flirted with him, and never once mentioned Josie's name to him.

I was a bad friend.

As I went through the rest of the evening, I tried to push away my guilt. Before I got into bed, I decided to make a list of ten reasons why it wasn't wrong to talk with Ethan.

1. Manners. It's just polite to talk to someone when they phone you.
2. You can't dictate who a guy likes. It's not my fault Josie flung herself down the escalator and made a bad impression on him.
3. I've liked Ethan for almost as long as Josie, so why should she have dibs on him just because her crush got a jump start on mine?
4. Why should Josie hold it against me if a guy likes me? I don't hold it against Josie that she's better at school and basketball—well, at least not much. Okay, I do hold it against her. Cross out number 4 on this list.
5. Ethan is way cute.
6. Ditto for reasons number 6–10.

There was no way around it. I was a bad friend. The next time I spoke to Ethan, I would talk about nothing except all the ways Josie was a wonderful person, and then I'd ask my parents if I was too young to become a nun.

Seven

Josie

I rode my bike to the school the next day. I didn't bring anything but paper and pencil. Frederick had all the rocket supplies, guarding them at his house like they were made of diamonds instead of cardboard tubes and plastic fins. When I rode up, he was setting up a launchpad in the middle of the football field. He gave me a rundown of the procedures, as though he were the teacher and I were his student, then ended his speech with, "I'll record the flight time and flight path in my notebook and keep it at my house."

"Fine." I picked up one of the rockets to look at the fins, but he grabbed it from me like he expected me to snap it in two.

"These aren't toys." He laid the rocket down by the other three on the ground. "I'll set them off."

I picked up the video camera from his pile of stuff on the ground. "Okay. I'll video the rockets in flight then."

He took the video camera from my hands. "I'll do that too."

"You'll set them off, videotape them, and record the data? What am I supposed to do?"

"You can retrieve the rockets once they hit the ground."

"Retrieve them? Like a dog?"

"Right. You're an athlete, so running should be no problem for you."

I forced a smile. "Yeah, but you're not an athlete, so you need the exercise." I took the video camera back from him and looked at the buttons. "Besides, you can't ignite the rockets and tape their flights. It just makes more sense if I tape them flying and you run after them."

He held his hand out for the camera. "You're not taping the flights. I know what you'll do. You'll video me chasing after the rockets and make a stupid commentary about how I run like a girl, or zoom in on my butt or something."

"Frederick, why would I want to see a close-up of your butt?"

He kept holding his hand out for the video camera. "Just give me the camera. I'm not letting you ruin my science project."

"Ruin it? You're not even letting me touch it, and it's supposed to be *our* science project."

He took the video camera from my hands. "Yeah, well, I know what I'm doing, and you don't."

I thought about grabbing one of the rockets and holding it hostage until he gave the camera back to me, but decided to reason with him one more time before I resorted to violence against cardboard tubes. I held my hand out to him. "I can work a camera, Frederick. It isn't that hard. You push the button and point."

He glanced from the rockets to me, fingering the camera like it was his firstborn child. "Well, all right. But no commentaries."

After he handed me the camera, he picked up the first rocket and strode over to the launchpad. "Hey, Frederick," I called after him. "You walk like a girl."

"Shut up," he called back.

All in all, we were getting along better than I expected.

We set off each of the four rockets, replaced the rocket motors, and set them off again. The ones with the good fins flew in high arcs above the football field, so high sometimes it was hard to tell which direction they were going. The two with the cutoff fins went up a few feet, then spiraled out of control, turning nose over bottom like a fiery pinwheel. We made a total of eight flights and recovered all but one rocket. It flew into a yard in a neighborhood by the school, and although we crawled over a cinder-block wall to get it, we were prevented from accomplishing this mission by two Scottish terriers who had other ideas about the space program. I did get some great footage of Frederick scaling the block wall while wearing a terrier on his pant leg, though.

When we made it back to the football field and sat on the grass, panting, I showed it to him using the replay button. "Look, I think you can see the fingernail marks from where you clawed your way up the wall."

"Yeah, and thanks for helping me fend off the dogs."

"It's your science project, I knew you'd want to be the one who took the teeth in the leg for rocketry."

"I'll be sure to mention that in our oral report. I'm the one who took the teeth."

I turned off the camera and set it on my lap. "We jocks may not be smart enough to figure out rocket science, but we can outrun the dogs. They pick off the sick and the weak first, you know."

He lay down on the grass, his arms splayed out. "You're going to tell everyone at school about this, aren't you?"

"Tell? Of course not. I'm going to distribute copies of the video—"

He sat up and grabbed the video camera away from me. "I'm erasing it right now." He pushed the rewind button, then pointed the camera at the grass. "There went your chance to humiliate me in front of everyone. Are you happy now?"

I lay down, feeling the grass prickle my back through my shirt. My breath was finally coming in a normal rhythm. "Geez, Frederick, I was only joking. Don't you have a sense of humor?"

He put the lens cap back on the camera. "Oh, yeah. I have a wonderful sense of humor, and I think it's hilarious every time one of you jocks gives me a wedgie during PE. I just can't stop laughing every time I'm shoved into a locker."

I sat up on my elbows in the grass. "I have never given anyone a wedgie during PE."

"No, you're right. Girls don't give wedgies, they call names. 'Hey, there goes Frederick the Whine. The Wino. Would you like a little wine with your dinner? No? Neither would we, so just bottle it, Frederick, and maybe one day you'll be vintage and worth something. Ha ha.' You girls are so funny."

"I've never said any of that to you, Frederick." Although, now that I thought about it, I may have been the one who started the whole vintage comment behind his back.

He gathered up the three rockets we had left and shoved them into his backpack. He took his notebooks and did the same.

"I'm sorry I was teasing you," I said, because I felt like I should say something. His face had a pinched look to it as he gathered up all of his supplies, and suddenly I did feel sorry that people teased him. "I won't tell anyone about the dog. Really. I mean, stuff like that happens to me all the time. Two days ago I tripped down an up escalator."

He didn't answer me, just put the last of his pencils and paper in his backpack and slid it onto his shoulders. "We'll need to write up the report and then get together to lay out the science fair board."

"Okay."

He got on his bike without saying good-bye and pedaled using standing strides. I got on my bike and rode back to my house, considerably slower. I had never thought twice about calling Frederick "the Whine," but hearing him repeat all of it back to me, well, it made my stomach feel like I'd been eating lead.

Cami

Ethan called me twice over the weekend. He teased me about having stuffed animals in my room, and having a thing for cartoon men. We talked about English class, writing poems, and basketball. Then we talked about basketball poems. (Okay, there aren't any, but there should be. I considered writing one entitled "Dribble, Dribble, It's not Just Drivel.")

I never said anything to him about Josie. Somehow I couldn't. For once I wasn't second-best in someone's opinion. I felt special. Important. I didn't want to jinx it by telling him Josie liked him too.

On Monday, while I stood at my locker getting stuff out for first period, Ethan handed me a Snickers bar. "It's for Kevin. You know, payoff for telling me your deepest, darkest secrets."

"Right. Like I'm going to give him this for ratting on me about Jackie Chan." I opened the candy bar and took a bite.

"Hey," Ethan said. "Now your brother will think I'm a deadbeat who doesn't pay his candy-bar debts."

"Poor you." I took another bite.

I didn't hear Josie walk up behind me until she stood right by my shoulder. "Hi, Cami. Hi, Ethan."

I swallowed part of the Snickers bar wrong and started to choke.

"Are you okay?" Josie asked me.

I nodded and coughed.

"That's what you get for eating someone else's ill-gotten gains," Ethan said.

"What?" Josie asked.

"It wasn't her candy bar," Ethan said. "It was Kevin's."

I coughed harder, finally finding my voice. "Funny, Snickers just aren't as good when they go down your lungs. I'll have to try eating it next time."

"So why do you have Kevin's candy bar?" Josie asked, smiling at Ethan and not at me.

"Because you can never have too much chocolate in the morning." I had no idea what I was saying. I just wanted to keep Ethan from telling Josie anything, like the fact he'd called me. "That's why so many people enjoy Cocoa Puffs. A great cereal. Little sugar balls in chocolate milk. What more could you ask from a meal?"

"Taste," Ethan said.

"Nutrition," Josie said.

I shoved the half-eaten candy bar into my locker. "Well, I guess if you're picky about your breakfast, then technically, yeah, you might want something with taste and nutrition. What did you two have for breakfast?"

"Raisin Bran," Josie said.

"Total," Ethan said.

"Then you're both flaky people."

Ethan swatted my shoulder with his notebook. "Who are you calling flaky?"

"I mean people who eat flakes. Flake-eaters."

He gave me a killer smile. "Yeah, I knew what you meant. See you later."

Josie and I both watched him turn and walk down the hallway.

"That doesn't count as my third conversation with Ethan, does it?" Josie asked.

"Well, you talked to him, didn't you?"

"Yeah, but I'm not sure telling him what I ate for breakfast actually constitutes a conversation." She sighed and held her books to her chest. "Ethan actually touched you with his notebook and then smiled at you. I wish I had thought to call him flaky."

"You can tell him he's flaky another time."

She walked slowly down the hallway, her long brown hair swishing against her back. "Ethan has the greatest smile. I would just die if he ever asked me out."

That made two of us. I'd die if he asked out Josie too.

I'd have to tell her sometime that he'd called me, and more important, I'd have to tell her I liked him, but I had no idea how. I just wanted to put it off for as long as possible.

Josie

It's hard to write poetry when you have siblings. I bet Shakespeare was an only child. Every time I put down three words, someone barges into my room to talk to me.

First line of poetry: *There's more than meets the eye to me.*

This was a good first line because it should have been a snap to come up with something to rhyme with *me*. I mean, the dictionary is full of words ending in the long *e* sound. *Gee, see, be, free, key, he, knee, tree, we,* and anything that has *y* or *ly* on the end, like *really easy.* Only it wasn't. Really easy, I mean.

My homework session:

Kristen pops into my room: Have you seen my blue shirt?

Me: No. Go away. I'm composing poetry.

Hopefully, happily, regretfully, casually, dramatically . . . Am I dramatic?

Sadie comes into my room: Is Jack in here? He took my karaoke machine, and I'm going to kill him.

Me: No. Go away. I'm composing poetry.

I hear noises from a karaoke machine and Jack singing in the hallway. Jack is not singing any actual tune; he's just making things up.

Jack: Sadie is ugly, and she's smelly too. If she could growl like an ape, we'd trade her to the zoo.

It figures. My five-year-old brother wasn't having any trouble rhyming words, but I can't come up with something to rhyme with *me.*

> *There's more than meets the eye to me,*
> *But will I ever be noticed by he?*

Nope. The words are in the wrong order—besides, it makes me sound pathetic, which maybe I am, but it's better not to admit it to my entire English class.

Sadie screaming in the hallway: Jack, give me back my karaoke machine right now!

Jack gives a shriek that is amplified by the microphone, then runs into my room.

Jack: Save me!

Me: No. Go away. I'm composing poetry.

Jack holds on to the microphone with one hand and my bedpost with the other.

Jack: Josie! Josie! Josie!

Mom's voice from downstairs: Josie, leave your brother alone!

Me yelling back: I'm not doing anything. I'm just trying to compose something for school, but I can't because everyone keeps bothering me!

Mom: You're composting? I thought you were doing rockets for your science project. If you're going to compost, you'd better do it outside. I don't want you making a mess in your room.

I toss down my notebook and go outside to shoot hoops. If I can't think of anything to write by the time the assignment is due, I'll ask Jack for help.

Cami

Over the next few days Ethan made a habit of speaking to me at my locker, especially if Ashley was around. I didn't mind that he became more talkative when she was nearby. It was sort of fun to see her lips contort into all sorts of grimaces while she pretended not to listen to us. I wanted to smile over at her and say, "I guess popularity can't buy you everything, can it? Your ex-boyfriend is interested in me now." But I never did—well, at least not out loud. Maybe Ashley had the psychic "gift" Caroline was trying to develop, though, because she glared at me like she knew what I was thinking.

Ethan and I discussed our homework assignments, teachers—nothing important, and yet it all seemed so important to me. His opinions could have been carved in stone and set next to the Ten Commandments just because he was Ethan Lancaster.

He called me on Tuesday night, and Wednesday night. I wanted to be home Thursday night, but I had an appointment to go stare at people at the library with Caroline.

We sat at a table in the corner, notebooks open, a stopwatch between us, staring at the patrons. Some of them never looked over at us. Which was fine as far as I was concerned, because then I didn't have to look away quickly and pretend I'd been staring at something else. Half of our subjects glanced back at us in under a minute. Caroline was thrilled by this. "See, they're using their sixth sense."

"Maybe they're just looking around."

"You're such a cynic." She tilted her chin down at me. "I think this experiment would work better if you could put out a more positive aura."

"And I think this experiment would work better if we took it somewhere else. The librarian is starting to look over at us even when we're not staring at her."

Caroline flipped shut her notebook. "Fine. I'm getting hungry anyway. Let's ride our bikes to a fast-food place. There are always plenty of people at those."

We rode three blocks to McDonald's, then chained our bikes together because there wasn't a bike rack around. I wasn't entirely comfortable with this solution, because I had a two-hundred-and-eighty-dollar Schwinn; so if someone wanted to steal my bike, it just meant they got to have Caroline's too, as a bonus. While we ordered, I kept glancing out the window to make sure no one was hefting them into the back of their truck. Caroline ordered a salad. She didn't eat meat because, as she told me, animals have consciousness too. I wanted a hamburger but didn't want to be lectured while I ate it, so I bought a large order of fries and a shake. We settled into the booth closest to the door and took out the stopwatch and our notebooks.

First subject: A child playing in the ball pit and on the slides. We timed her for three minutes. She never looked at us or, for that matter, at her mother, who kept calling to her that it was time to go.

Second subject: The mother. She didn't look at us either. We timed her for five minutes, which was the amount of time it took for her to crawl into the ball pit and retrieve her daughter.

Third subject: The remaining boy in the ball pit. He looked at the slides, the balls, the windows, the tables, but never at us. We stopped timing him after two and half minutes because he was picking his nose, and we didn't want to watch that.

"See," I told Caroline. "It's not working. People can't tell when you stare at them."

"That's because you're not really trying. You keep looking over at your bike. You're not concentrating."

"Hey, it's not my psychic powers that are being tested, it's theirs. And apparently they don't have any."

She took a bite of her salad and shook her head. "Maybe

children aren't tuned into their sixth sense yet. Let's try those girls who just walked in."

Three teenage girls picked up their order from the counter and sauntered back to the tables. They were probably high school dropouts, or gang members, or perhaps recent parolees. One had dyed-black hair that spiked straight up. Another wore a necklace that looked like a dog collar; the third had purple lipstick and the beefy arms of a sumo wrestler.

"Let's not stare at them," I said.

Caroline took a bite of her salad. "What are you worried about? I thought you didn't think this stuff worked. If you're right, they won't notice us staring at all."

I leaned over the table toward her and lowered my voice. "No, I'm pretty sure they're used to being stared at, and they probably don't like it."

"Don't be ridiculous. People only dress that way because they want other people to stare at them. I'll start the stopwatch." She pressed the button, laid the watch down on the table, and took another bite of her salad.

I slunk down in my seat and nibbled at my fries. I didn't want to stare at the girls, but I couldn't help myself. My gaze was riveted on them the same way it turned to car wrecks on the road.

Spiky Hair lit up a cigarette. A guy behind the counter walked over and told them they couldn't smoke inside the restaurant. She dipped her fingers in her soda, then used them to snuff out her cigarette. As the guy walked back to the counter, she flipped him off.

"Do you think she'll drink her soda after putting her fingers in it?" Caroline asked. "Gross."

"Shhh. Keep your voice down."

"Of course, she just had her lips on a cigarette, so I guess she's not too picky about what goes into her mouth. Smoking is *so* disgusting."

"Shhh, Caroline."

The girl with the purple lips and sumo-wrestler arms turned around in her seat to look at us. "Do you have something to say?" she barked out.

"Who, us?" I asked. "No. We're just finishing up our meal."

"Then why don't you put your eyes back where they belong and stop looking over here?"

Caroline stopped the timer, then picked up her pencil and made a notation in her notebook. "We're doing a science project on the sixth sense, and staring at people is part of it. You're the first people at this sitting to realize we were staring, but it took you three minutes and forty-two seconds, so I'm not sure what that says about your psychic powers."

Sumo Girl put one hand on the table and leaned forward, the muscles in her beefy arm flexing. "You want to see psychic powers? Then how about this—I'll think about what I'm going to do to your face thirty seconds from now, and you see if you can read my mind."

Suddenly I realized I had psychic powers, or at least a very vivid imagination. I stood up and grabbed my backpack. "We're leaving now."

Caroline didn't move. "You're going to let those girls chase you out of McDonald's?"

"No, that's what's going to happen in thirty seconds if we don't leave now. Come on."

She shoved the notebook and watch into her backpack, then followed me outside. "We had as much right to be in McDonald's as they did. And at least staring at people doesn't contribute to lung cancer."

I undid my chain and got on my bike, glad it hadn't been stolen. This was the one bright moment in an afternoon spent with a partner who should have been concentrating on basic mind functions, such as self-preservation, instead of psychic powers. "Caroline, I think we should choose another science project to do. I don't want to stare at people anymore."

She slipped onto her bike and snapped her helmet in place. "You know what your problem is?" She didn't give me time to answer, which was too bad because at that moment I could have given her quite a rundown. "Your problem is, you don't believe in ESP. You're too skeptical. Would Henry Ford have ever invented the car if he didn't believe it would work?"

I pedaled my bike from the parking lot onto the sidewalk, with Caroline riding beside me. "Henry Ford didn't invent the car. He just mass-produced it."

"Well, there you have it. Maybe he would have invented it if he had believed it would work in the first place."

"Fine. I think you have a great point. Let's invent a car for our science project. I believe in those."

She pulled ahead of me on her bike. "We're doing the sixth sense. You already agreed to it. We'll get together later to collect more data; right now I just want to go home, where the feng shui is better." She pedaled faster, going off down the sidewalk, and farther ahead.

I stared at her, but she never looked back at me. Some sixth sense she had.

Eight

Josie

I decided to help Cami with her science project by staring at Ethan in English class. It was easy to do, and if he looked back at me, I could tell him I wasn't a pathetic, love-struck groupie; I was a scientist.

He didn't look back.

Ashley must have seen me staring at him though, and she knew exactly what it meant. Girls always do.

As I walked to the gym after school she came up beside me wearing one of her phony smiles. "So, Josie, are you ditching Frederick for Ethan?"

I pretended I didn't know what she was talking about. "No—I didn't even know Ethan needed a science fair partner."

"I meant as a boyfriend. I know Ethan pretty well, so if you're interested in him, I could give you some pointers."

Yeah, right. The only thing with a point Ashley had ever wanted to give me was a knife in the back. She was just looking for some new way to bother me, and I didn't want to give her the satisfaction. I stared down the hall and judged the time it would take me to make it to the gym. Probably another minute. Could I completely ignore her until then?

"Of course, you could ask Cami about Ethan if you wanted," Ashley went on. "She knows him really well. She's always flirting and throwing herself at him when they're at their lockers together."

So Ashley's new way to bother me wasn't to razz me about Ethan, it was to try and turn me against Cami. Like that was going to work. Ashley should have known I'd never believe anything she told me.

I put on a phony smile of my own. "Thanks, Ashley. If I ever need advice on how to attract a guy, I'll ask Cami. But if I need advice on how to dump one, I'll ask you. That's where your expertise lies."

Ashley grunted, shook her head like she couldn't believe how immature I was, and pulled ahead of me so we weren't walking side by side anymore.

Which all in all saved me about thirty seconds of having to put up with her. I didn't consider it a loss.

That night, before our first game against Ajo, Coach Melbourne tried to hype us up in the locker room. We sat on the benches in crisp red and blue uniforms while she stood in front of us holding a new autographed Rebecca Lobo poster in a glass frame.

"One day I could be putting a poster of you up," she told us, "but do you know what that will take on your part?"

Growing three inches, and a good agent.

"Work," Coach Melbourne said, "and then more work. I

want to see some of that work right now." She tapped the glass frame. "Do you know how I'll choose a girl to help Rebecca with her demonstration? She'll be the one out there working her legs, her arms, and her heart out." She gazed over the group of us, giving a moment for this emphasis to sink in. "It's a big honor. Not many girls will ever be able to say they met a WNBA player, let alone played with one." More tapping on the glass. For someone who didn't have long fingernails, Coach Melbourne could get a lot of noise out of a picture frame. "The whole town will be there. Your picture will be in the *Sanchez Herald*. Maybe some of the bigger papers like the *East Valley Tribune* and *Arizona Republic* will pick up the story. Maybe a news station or two. That's quite a nice souvenir for a little work, don't you think?"

I hadn't considered the whole newspaper/TV aspect of this wager. I hadn't thought through the fact that our whole town would be watching the high scorer play with Rebecca Lobo.

Suddenly it was so easy to see myself there in the gym, walking toward Rebecca while flash bulbs went off around me. The audience would explode with applause, and everyone would know that although I'm not sophisticated and "in," I'm good at something. I've got game.

My parents would be so proud, they'd send out newspaper clippings to all of the relatives and brag about me in the next Christmas card. At school everyone would congratulate me and ask me what it was like to meet Rebecca Lobo. I'd be a celebrity. I bet even Ethan would come up and talk to me. That was the third conversation I wanted, wasn't it?

I glanced over to where Cami sat, listening to Coach Melbourne go on about the effort she expected from us when we played Ajo. Cami's face was utter concentration. She was probably already the ball, just waiting to spring toward the basket.

But I could be the high-scoring player if I tried, and wouldn't that make Coach Melbourne choose me as the most valuable player?

What exactly had been the wording of Cami's and my agreement? For me to try not to be high scorer, I was supposed to have three conversations with Ethan—but I hadn't. I mean, saying two words about breakfast cereal doesn't equal a conversation, and when you came right down to it, the time at the mall wasn't much of a conversation either. It had mostly been just Cami and I denying we were any relation to Jack.

Besides, it wouldn't be right for me to try *not* to score during a game. Our team depended on me. Certainly Cami understood that. I would feed the ball to her when I could, but it was my duty to make as many points for the team as I could.

Ten minutes later we ran out into the gym while the cheerleaders chanted, "Go, Sanchez Eagles!" and the few rows of parents clapped.

It was time to play.

Cami

Coach Melbourne stood on the sidelines for most of the game, clapping her hands at us as we ran by, yelling, "Hustle, girls!"

So I hustled.

I haven't run so hard since that day when I was ten years

old walking home from school with Kevin. He told me a busload of insane criminals had escaped somewhere near Sanchez—and then his best friend, Carson, jumped out from the bushes at me, waving his arms and screaming.

Probably no ten-year-old has ever run so fast—and that was running after, not away from, Carson and Kevin. I might have caught them if I hadn't been wearing flip-flops.

Anyway, by the end of the game I almost expected my lungs to crawl out of my throat and surrender. And I still wasn't high scorer. I made a good number of rebounds and assists, but my layups were off, and my free throws were pathetic.

Josie made twenty points, and Ashley made twelve. I'd only made nine. I knew, because during the game I kept better track of our points than I did of the Red Raiders' score. It only vaguely sank in we'd won. Winning somehow didn't matter, just being high scorer did.

Afterward, I lay down on one of the benches in the locker room with a wet towel across my forehead while I tried to convince my lungs to stay put. Josie walked by me, head tipped back, a water bottle to her lips. She drank so quickly some of the water drizzled down her chin. Smiling, she waved the water bottle in my direction. "Good game, Camilla. I think your free throws are getting better. You actually made one today."

"Yeah, but I missed the other one."

She shrugged. "Nobody's perfect."

"You came pretty close." I moved the towel from my forehead to my neck and checked to make sure no one else was close by. "Twenty points. You really took my directions about not letting Ashley be high scorer to heart, didn't you?"

She nodded and took another drink of water. "Oh, sure. I know how much Ashley bugs you."

"Right. Thanks."

"No problem."

I moved the towel from my neck back to my forehead. "Next game you could pass me a few more balls."

"I'll try, but you'll have to run faster to get open."

I put my hand on my chest to make sure my lungs were still there. "I'll run faster."

I pictured myself walking up to Rebecca Lobo, just like I had pictured the scene a hundred times before, but this time Rebecca didn't look at me. This time Rebecca looked over my shoulder at Josie.

Josie

I changed into my normal clothes and shoved my sweaty basketball uniform into my duffel bag. Ideally, I would remember to wash it before the next game. Last year I hardly ever remembered to unpack my duffel bag, and then a couple of hours before the game I was washing out my uniform in the sink and hoping I didn't have to start the game wearing damp shorts.

Out on the court, my parents stood talking to Cami's parents as they waited for us to come out of the locker room. My dad saw me first and waved. "There's my superstar.

Twenty points." He turned to my mom. "She's a chip off the old block, exactly like me."

"Definitely," Mom said. "Except I think twenty points was what you scored during your entire basketball career."

Mom and Dad both laughed at this. Come to think of it, they laugh at a lot of things, which is probably where I got my tendency to giggle for no reason. I inherited their laughing disorder.

Cami's mother smiled over at me. "You did very well tonight, Josie."

"Thanks." I felt pinpricks of guilt and couldn't look at her. It was supposed to be Cami who did well tonight—and maybe she would have if I'd passed the ball to her more. Instead I'd kept the ball and made the shots myself.

Cami's dad said, "Great three-pointer in the second half. You scored more than anyone."

"Yeah, um, Cami will be right out. She wanted to cool down a little before she dressed." I couldn't stay here another moment and talk with Cami's parents. I handed my duffel bag to Mom. "Can you take this? I want to get another drink before we leave."

Halfway to the drinking fountain, Caroline intercepted me. "Hey, Josie, did Cami leave already?"

"No, she's still in the locker room."

"Oh, good. I want to talk to her. I decided to come to the game and stare at people. I got some great data, plus this cute guy asked for my phone number." She fingered her notebook and smiled wistfully. "He saw me staring and figured I was interested. Did I pick the greatest science project, or what?"

"It beats my rocket project. So far, the only guy who's asked for my phone number is Frederick."

She tucked her notebook into her backpack. "You can learn a lot by staring at people, by studying their karma. I'm practicing to be a psychic, you know." Then Caroline looked at me with a penetrating gaze.

She was trying to see into my mind—to see how I was planning to take away Rebecca Lobo from my best friend.

I wanted to bolt away from her, to bolt out of the gym altogether. "Great. Well, see you later." I hurried past her to the drinking fountain.

I was a bad friend.

A very bad friend.

Next game I'd pass the ball to Cami every chance I got. I'd make sure she was the high-scoring player if I had to rip the ball out of Ashley's hands to do so.

Cami

List of bad things that happened at the basketball game:

1. Josie was high scorer.
2. Ashley was second high scorer.
3. My lungs have probably been permanently scarred from panting so hard.
4. My brother asked Caroline for her phone number. If they start going out and I have to watch her snuggle up to Kevin and murmur things about good karma, I will become physically ill.

It doesn't matter to him that she's considering spending her adult life trying to communicate with canaries or that she's trying to force me into staring at people for our science project. He thinks she's "hot."

What strange and warped criteria do guys use when they decide to like a girl?

Ethan didn't call me over the weekend, but on both Monday and Tuesday he brought me a Snickers bar to give to Kevin. I took a bite out of them in front of Ethan just to show him I wouldn't let my brother be his informant. When Ethan brought me another one on Wednesday, I told him, "Kevin would like a Reese's Peanut Butter Cup for a change."

Ethan leaned around his locker and smiled at me. "For Reese's Peanut Butter Cups, I need to know more secrets. I need to know the mysteries of womanhood, like why they take so long in the bathroom every morning."

"That's when we go over our handbooks for how to take over the world."

"I thought so."

On Thursday he brought me Reese's Peanut Butter Cups. I shared one with him, but still felt guilty he'd given me so many candy bars. After practice I rode my bike to Walgreens and bought him five Snickers bars. I figured I would sneak one a day into his locker.

I spent twenty minutes trying to write the perfect note to go along with the first candy bar. Something cute, but not pushy.

Ethan,
This is for your older sister as payment for telling me all your
deep, dark secrets. If you don't have any deep, dark secrets, I'll
settle for a few shallow, dimly lit secrets. Have her give me a
call. You already know the number,
Cami

Fifteen of the twenty minutes were spent deciding whether to write "Love, Cami" or just "Cami." I decided to skip the "love" because we weren't officially going out. Yet. But certainly he'd ask me out soon. I mean, you didn't bring a girl candy bars every day and then not ask her out.

I wanted him to ask me out almost as badly as I didn't want him to ask me out. Once he asked me out, I'd have to tell Josie about it, and I dreaded that.

The next morning I put the candy bar and note on the top of my books in my backpack so it wouldn't get squashed, and wondered if he'd eat it in front of me when he found it.

When I got to school, Josie came through the front door the same time I did, and we walked up to my locker together. As I spun my combination, she leaned against the locker next to mine and tossed her hair off her shoulder. She'd been trying to copy Ashley's "sophisticated moves" lately. Josie nearly had it down, though I couldn't see why she wanted to copy Ashley in the first place. If you ask me, Ashley looks like some sort of horse when she swings her hair everywhere.

Josie ran her hand across her hair to smooth it down from where she'd messed it up. "Did you get your poem done for English?"

"Well, I wrote one entitled 'The Science Fair Project, a Near-Death Experience,' but I'm not sure I want to recite it in front of everybody. It isn't very good. You know, everything sounds stupid when you rhyme it."

"You didn't really do a poem about staring at people in McDonalds, did you?"

"Yes, I did." I cleared my throat, then realized I couldn't think of my opening stanza. I opened my locker and waved one hand at her. "Okay, I forget the first part, but the last part goes,

'Then sumo girl got in my face,
and told me I'd better leave this place.
Adios, Ronald. Good-bye, McFry.
I'm Mc-splitting before I die.' "

Josie laughed, but tried to stop herself by covering her mouth with her hand. "I don't think the rhyming had much to do with it sounding stupid."

"Hey, I never claimed to be Robert Frost."

"Which is a good thing, since you can be arrested for identify theft these days."

I opened my backpack to unload my books, and as I did, the candy bar fell out. It rolled over on the ground and lay at Josie's feet like a stick of dynamite. Josie picked it up, started to hand it back to me, and then saw the name on the note.

"Ethan? What's this?"

I grabbed the candy bar from her. With trembling hands I thrust it into my locker. "Nothing. I was just going to put this in his locker, you know, because he's given me some candy bars."

"Why has he given you candy bars?"

I had to tell her sooner or later about Ethan and me, and later was very quickly becoming now, but I still didn't want to do it. I stood in front of my locker, feeling shaky, and looked at my books, not her.

"What's going on between you two?" she asked.

I took out my math book for first period, then shut the locker door. "Listen, Josie, I've been meaning to talk to you about this, but I didn't want to hurt your feelings. Ethan has called me a few times. I think he's going to ask me to go out with him, at least I hope he is. I've liked him for a long time."

She took a step backward, as though I'd hit her. The color drained from her face. "You stole Ethan from me?"

"No, I didn't *steal* him, because it's not like he was ever going out with you."

"Oh, that makes it okay then, doesn't it?" She spun around and hurried away without letting me answer.

"Josie!" I called after her, but she walked faster, until her backpack blended into the stream of students flowing down the hallway.

I'd meant to explain it more gently to her. I'd meant to give her my entire list of reasons why it wasn't my fault Ethan had been calling me.

But then perhaps it was for the best I didn't give her my reasons. After seeing her face, none of them seemed like good reasons anyway.

Nine

Josie

I felt numb. My feet were slapping against the floor, but they didn't feel connected to me. Tears pressed against the back of my eyes. I tried to keep them from coming. A person just didn't cry walking down the hallway to first period. Crying was something you did alone in your room when you were a little kid. I couldn't cry now.

I walked into the bathroom, went into a stall, and leaned against the wall, taking small shallow breaths, but the tears came down my cheeks anyway.

It wasn't that Ethan didn't like me, although that hurt too. I just couldn't believe Cami had gone behind my back and taken him. She knew I liked him. She was supposed to be helping me attract him, not sabotaging me so she could have him. What had she done?

Ashley told me Cami had been flirting and throwing herself at him. Who would have ever thought Ashley told me the truth and Cami deceived me? How long had this been going on, and who else knew about it?

In my mind I saw the entire student body watching me, whispering about it. They'd all seen me run into the bathroom, and now they were saying to one another, "Well, Cami finally broke the news to her. Did you see her face? How pathetic."

The bell for first period rang. I stood in the stall, fingering my backpack strap. I couldn't go to class. It would be obvious to everyone I'd been crying. I would just stay here till my eyes cleared up, then I'd go down to the office and tell them I was sick and needed to go home.

I listened to the few remaining footsteps hurrying off down the hallway until the school was silent.

If I left now, what would Cami think? She would know how upset I'd been. She'd tell Ethan about it.

I took a wad of toilet paper from the dispenser and wiped my cheeks. I wasn't going home. Cami would never know how I felt about this, or anything else. She wasn't my friend anymore. Apparently she hadn't been for a long time. She'd traded my friendship for Ethan's.

I hoped he would dump her as soon as possible. In fact, if I could do anything to hurry that event along, I would.

I left the stall and walked to the sink. Turning on the faucet, I splashed cold water on my face until my eyes didn't feel like they were burning anymore. I practiced smiling in the mirror, shrugging my shoulders as though I was talking to someone. No one would know how I felt if I could fake being normal until this stopped hurting. I smiled again. I'd do it. I had to.

Cami

I waited outside of Josie's first-period class until the bell rang. She never came. I walked slowly to my math class, repeating over and over all the things I wanted to say to her. *I've liked him for nearly as long as you have. I just never went on and on about it because I'm the type of person who keeps those things inside. So how come your liking him takes precedence over my liking him? Are you the only one who's allowed to have crushes on guys? Just because I got lucky this time and you didn't, that somehow makes me the bad one? I didn't run off and not speak to you when you got put in honors math and science and I didn't. I didn't run off in eighth grade when you made the A basketball team and I only made the B squad. Where is it written that you get everything you want, and I have to be content to stay in your shadow?*

But mostly I wanted to tell her, *Look, I didn't mean to hurt you.*

As I took the last few steps to class, my head felt like it had cracked open. I wished I had some Tylenol in my locker, but I didn't. No one did. With our school's zero-tolerance drug policy, we couldn't even bring Tic Tacs into the building for fear a teacher would see us pop one into our mouth and drag us down to see the principal.

I didn't have time to go to the health office, so I'd just have to live with the pain until I could talk to Josie. Once I made her see things my way, I'd feel better.

Josie

I did a good job of faking happy when I went to first period. Perhaps too good of a job. I just smiled when the algebra teacher gave me a tardy pass and told me I'd have to go down to the office and have myself un–marked absent.

I smiled all through the hallway and at the office staff. I smiled so much they started looking at me suspiciously. Students are supposed to look penitent when they have a tardy pass in their hands.

On the way back to class, I passed Ethan's locker. He was standing in front of it, getting his books out. His hair was even more mussed than usual. All the nervousness I'd felt around him before evaporated. He didn't like me, so what did it matter how I acted? Without knowing exactly why I was doing it, I stopped in front of his locker, the fake smile still plastered on my lips. "You're even later than I am." I waved my tardy pass at him and mimicked the attendance secretary's voice. "It's time to start taking your education seriously."

He grabbed a pencil from his locker shelf. "I slept through my alarm. I've been up for about three minutes."

"That would explain why your shirt is on backward."

He looked down at his shirt with panic, then saw I was joking and let out a sigh. "You had me going there. I ran out of the house so quickly, anything is possible. I had bread for breakfast. I didn't even have time to toast it. I'm going to be starving by second period."

No, he wouldn't. Cami had brought him a candy bar. She

must not have put it in his locker yet, or he'd know. The thought of that candy bar gave me a sharp pain in my stomach. I wanted to get even with her, and I could.

He shut his locker door and walked alongside me as we went down the hallway. "I think it's great that you're going out with Cami," I said. "It's important for her to have people who support her now."

"We're not going out. We're just friends." His gaze swung over to me. "And what do you mean, support her?"

"You know, through her probation." I tilted my head at him. "You did know she's a kleptomaniac, didn't you?"

"A klepto-what?"

I waved one hand as though it were nothing. "Someone who compulsively steals things. Only she's trying to work through it, and her probation officer says it's important for her to build healthy relationships, so it's great the two of you are going out."

"We're not going out."

I giggled and patted him on the arm reassuringly. "Now don't let what I've said bother you. She's a great person, really, and she's only stolen from me once, so you probably have nothing to worry about."

He stopped walking. "She's stolen from you?"

"Just once." I shrugged. "Well, that I know of, anyway. You probably shouldn't give her the combination to your locker, to be on the safe side." I started walking down the hallway again, and he followed. "And when you go out on dates, I wouldn't go anywhere you could be arrested for shoplifting."

"We're not going out," he said again.

I laughed as though I knew he was joking. We came to my classroom, and I walked over and put my hand on the doorknob. "Well, it's been good talking to you. Really, I think you and Cami make the cutest couple. And by the way, you're wearing two different shoes."

Cami

Josie had Spanish second period and always went straight there from honors algebra. I didn't even bother trying to intercept her. I didn't have the time, and besides, maybe it was better to let her cool down for a while.

I went to my locker to exchange my algebra book for my basic-history-you-aren't-smart-enough-to-be-in-the-same-class-as-the-honors-kids book. While I was getting it out, I saw the candy bar sitting on top of my not-honors-either biology book.

The note didn't look cute anymore, and the whole thing seemed like a stupid idea. But I had it, and Josie had already seen it, so there was no point in not giving it to Ethan now. Besides, once he was joking around with me about our candy-for-secrets system, I'd feel better.

I took two steps over to his locker and twirled his combination. When I opened the door, a couple of Ethan's notebooks slid out onto the floor. Apparently he'd been in a hurry this morning and just shoved things in. I picked them up, unsure where they went or what to do with them. While

I was holding them, Ethan appeared by my side so quickly I jumped.

"What are you doing with my biology notebooks?" He grabbed them out of my hands as though I was going to contaminate them.

I felt myself blushing. "They fell out of your locker. I wasn't sure where you wanted them."

He shoved the notebooks back into his locker in a haphazard manner. "They just fell out? How did my locker get open?"

"I opened it. I was going to give you this." I handed him the candy bar.

He took it in his hands and turned it over suspiciously. "You were giving this to me?"

"Yes, it's a candy bar." Obviously it was a candy bar, but from the way he was examining it, you'd think it had explosives wired to it.

"Uh, thanks." He put the Snickers in his locker without reading the note. "How did you know my combination?"

"Safecracking is one of my hobbies." I smiled, but he didn't return my smile. Instead, his eyes narrowed. "The candy bar is for your sister," I went on. "So she'll be my informant. I figure it's only fair, since my brother told you all my secrets."

Ethan took out his math book. "Apparently he left out a few."

"Well, I hope so. My work for the CIA is top secret."

He still didn't smile. "I talked to Josie this morning. She told me about your klepping-thing."

"Klepping-thing?"

"You know, how you like to steal things."

I nearly dropped my history book. "She told you I steal things?"

He shut his locker door and edged away from me. "I hope you get it all worked out with your probation officer, and um, I think you're a nice girl and everything, but I just want to be friends."

I stared at him, mouth open, his words registering like pounding nails in my head. I couldn't even think of anything to say until he was retreating down the hallway. Then I yelled, "That's not true! I don't even have a probation officer!"

Several students turned around to stare at me. Ethan was not one of them.

I walked to history, fuming. I fumed through a lesson on the Declaration of Independence, and wrote a new poem for English while I wasn't fuming. Josie was not going to get away with this.

Ten

Josie

Cami was waiting for me outside the English room. Her arms were crossed tightly around her poetry book. Her lips were drawn in a thin line across her face. Apparently she and Ethan had spoken recently.

She stood in front of me as I neared the door. "You're going to tell Ethan the truth."

I put one hand on my hip. "Well, I could, but telling him you steal things was kinder than telling him what a backstabbing, two-timing friend you are."

"I'm backstabbing? Me? You told him I had a probation officer!"

"And you told me you'd get Ethan to notice me. I didn't think that meant while he was your boyfriend." I walked around her and went into the classroom. I was shaking as I took my seat. I hoped no one noticed. I couldn't look Ethan in the face, so I stared at his feet and his two unmatching shoes.

Brendan and Justin, who sat beside him, had each switched their shoes so they were wearing unmatching ones too. The entire side of the room seemed to be joking about it. Ashley kicked off her shoes, but before she could switch with anyone, Adam stole her shoe and pretended to be Prince Charming with it.

Ashley yelled, "Hey, give that back to me!" but you could tell by the way she pouted that she enjoyed the attention. She grabbed at her shoe, but Adam held it out of her reach and asked another girl, "Have you tried on the glass slipper yet?"

After a few moments of this, Ashley pulled her shoe away from Adam, but Brendan grabbed her other shoe and threw it to Adam. Adam missed, and it flew onto Frederick's desk.

He looked up from his science fiction novel, picked up the shoe, and threw it back to Ashley. "I'm trying to read over here. This is English, not PE."

"Right." Brendan intercepted the throw and waved the shoe at Frederick. "Because if this were PE, someone would have run your gym shorts up the flagpole by now."

Mrs. Detwiler walked through the door and clapped her hands to get our attention. "Class, sit down! Sit down, everyone."

People shuffled to their seats while she glanced up and down the rows, taking roll. When she finished, she sat on the edge of her desk with her grade book beside her. She smiled at us benevolently, like she was bestowing some favor. "Today we'll start reciting our personal poetry. Before you read, remember to tell us the title of the poem and what type of poem you're reading." She tugged at the scarf knotted around her neck, then folded her hands in her lap serenely. "Any volunteers to go first?"

Cami raised her hand.

Mrs. Detwiler nodded at her. "Please stand while reading, Cami."

Cami stood, glared at me, and then turned her attention to her paper.

"My poem is an AABB rhyme pattern and is titled 'Things That Tick Me Off about You.'" Another glance at me. The class fell silent as they watched her.

"Number one: Always, you must be the best.
You have to beat me in every test.
You shine in all the honors classes.
You get all the basketball passes.

Number two: Let's say you want a guy,
heaven forbid that another should try,
even in passing to get his attention.
You'll just come up with some lying invention.

This poem of mine could go quite long—
a detailed list of what you do wrong.
But to keep it short, here's what I'll do:
I'll tell you I'm done with number two."

Cami sat down. Everyone in the class stared at me. Mrs. Detwiler smiled uncomfortably. "Well, that was read very nicely, Cami. Would any one like to comment on assonance and alliteration in Cami's poem?"

Everyone looked at me. No one raised a hand.

I raised mine. Mrs. Detwiler nodded toward me. "You have a comment about the poetry, Josie?"

"No, I have my own poem to read."

Mrs. Detwiler tugged at her scarf again. "Very well. Please stand."

I stood and stared at Cami. "My poem is titled 'Oh, Yeah?' And it's free verse." I realized I wasn't holding a paper to read from, but it didn't matter. I spoke anyway. "It's fine with me if our friendship is done, because as a friend, you were a poor one." I hadn't meant to rhyme the first sentence, and now realized I'd have to do the same for the second.

"You say you're done being number two, but I don't see how that could be true." As long as I stuck with easy-to-rhyme words, I'd be all right.

"It seems to me number two fits you pretty well."

"Because"—*bell, sell, fell, gel*— "you're two-timing, two-faced, too selfish—and now everyone can tell."

I sat down. Everyone's gaze turned from me to Cami.

"Well," Mrs. Detwiler said. "Well . . ."

Cami raised her hand. "Mrs. Detwiler, I have a comment about Josie's poem."

Mrs. Detwiler stood back from her desk. "I think maybe we'll skip the comments on today's poems." She looked at me, back at Cami, then around the room furtively. "Who else would like to recite something for us? Did anyone write a sonnet?"

I didn't hear anyone else recite their poems. I had to write down my speech word for word so I could turn it in with my other poems. It wasn't hard to do. I remembered everything I'd said perfectly.

Cami

At lunchtime, instead of sitting with Josie at our regular table, I took my tray and sat with Tisha and Barbara from my history class. When they asked why I wasn't sitting with Josie, I told them, "Josie was jealous because a guy she liked called me, so she told him I had a criminal record." I also repeated this explanation to the four girls who came up to me during lunch and asked what the poems in English had been all about.

Josie sat with Rochelle and Raleigh from her advanced algebra class. She was probably telling them her version of how I'd stolen Ethan.

I hoped he would come up and talk to me. I wanted to prove to her that Ethan had seen through her lies. But he took his lunch and walked outside with Justin without even a glance at me. After hearing our poetry duel in English, he probably thought Josie and I were both insane.

Stupid poem. I still couldn't believe she'd said all of that to me. And knowing my luck, Mrs. Detwiler would give her a higher grade because it looked like she'd had hers "memorized."

All day I felt like people were silently taking sides. The girls who walked with Josie in the hall—her side. The girls who talked to me in class—my side, I hoped. The girls who passed the ball to her at basketball practice—her side. The girls who didn't pass the ball to me—her side.

I never used Ethan's name when I explained things to people—I wanted to keep him out of it as much as possible—but during a water break at practice Lucy Simmons asked me, "Are you going out with Ethan? Is that why you and Josie are fighting?"

So everyone had figured out it was Ethan anyway.

"No, we're not going out."

"Oh." Lucy took a drink of water. "But you are fighting with Josie?"

"Yeah."

"Oh. Sorry." She traipsed back onto the court to leave me wondering whose side she was on.

By the end of practice every nerve of mine had unraveled. There was no way I was going to ride home in a car with Josie. Her mother would ask why we weren't speaking to each other. As I passed by Josie in the locker room, I said, "I don't need a ride home."

She just shrugged. "Fine."

After I changed out of my practice clothes, I took my backpack, walked up to the office, and called my house to ask someone to pick me up. Kevin was the only one home, and he didn't have a car. So I waited for a few minutes until I knew Josie had already left, then walked the two miles home.

I wished I could have changed everything. I wished there was some way to undo everything so the two of us could just go back to how we'd been before today. But today had happened. Josie had hurt me. She'd done it on purpose, and she wasn't sorry for doing it. Things would never be the same again.

Josie

I don't think my mom was ever a teenager. How could she be, when she has absolutely no concept of what my life is like?

"You fought over a boy?" she asked when I told her why Cami wasn't riding home with us. She said this as though Cami and I had been fighting over broccoli. Mom tapped her fingers on the steering wheel. "There are hundreds of boys in your school. Do you really think one is worth more than your friendship with Cami?"

I folded my arms tightly across my chest. "First of all, there are hundreds of boys in the school, but they aren't interchangeable. I mean, only one of them is Ethan. Secondly, I wasn't the one who traded in our friendship—that was Cami—and thirdly, she isn't really gone. She lives on in my memory. Look, I've started making lists."

"Well, I think you two can work this out."

"Work it out? What do you suggest? She can lend me Ethan on the weekends? She can carry around a lie detector so I'll know when to trust her?"

Mom rolled her eyes. Jack leaned toward the front seat, putting his face close to my head. "Aren't you friends with Cami anymore?"

"No."

"I liked Cami."

"Figures. Apparently guys always like Cami best."

Cami

By the time I made it home, both my parents were in the kitchen putting sandwich stuff on the table. Mom loves submarine sandwiches because they involve no cooking. We have them once a week.

"You're home," Mom said. "We were wondering when you'd get here."

I put my backpack down by the door. My shoulders ached from carrying it the whole way. "I told Kevin I was walking."

Mom and Dad exchanged a look that let me know Kevin had also told them why I was walking. Mom took plates from the cupboard and set them on the table. "So are you planning on walking every day Josie's mom comes to pick you up? What about the days it's my turn to drive?"

I took a glass from the table and poured myself a big drink of water. "I don't want to carpool with Josie anymore."

Dad sat down at the table. Kevin and Mom joined him. "Wouldn't it be easier just to make up with Josie? You've been friends for a long time. You want to throw that all away?"

"It's already thrown away."

Kevin ripped open the package of rolls and took one out.

"So the guy liked you instead of Josie. You can't dictate who likes you. She can't blame you for that."

Dad took two rolls from the package and handed one to me. "Once Josie has time to cool off, she'll see things your way."

Mom poured herself a drink of water and didn't say anything. She was a teacher, and a girl. She knew better. She took a slow sip, then set her glass back on the table. "What am I supposed to tell Mrs. Caraway? I'm just supposed to call her up and say, 'Let's not carpool anymore'?"

"You don't have to. I'll talk to Josie about it," I said.

After dinner, I IM'd Josie.

> CamE: I think it would be best if we don't ride home
> from practice together anymore.
> JoC1: Fine.

That was all. I waited in front of the computer screen to see if she'd add anything. Something along the lines of: *Sorry I accused you of having a criminal past. Sorry I told the entire English class you were two-timing, two-faced, and selfish.* But she didn't write again.

I did my homework in my room, all the while half listening to see if Ethan would call. He didn't. At nine thirty at night I unwrapped two of the Snickers bars and cried while I ate them.

Eleven

Josie

The problem with hanging out with one best friend all the time is that when you get in a fight, you suddenly realize you have no other friends. Not really. As I walked through the halls of school on Monday, I saw lots of acquaintances, but no real friends. Not anyone who could finish a sentence for me. Not anyone I could bring to my house without straightening my room up first. How long did real friendships take to make?

I sat with Rochelle and Raleigh again at lunch and noticed that Rochelle clicked her tongue when she spoke. Neither of them played basketball. When I mentioned we had a game tonight against Buckeye, Raleigh said, "It's bad enough they make us play basketball in PE, I can't believe you stay after school to run up and down the court. I'd probably throw up if I had to do that."

Yep, here was someone I had a lot in common with.

I bet Ashley never found herself friendless. She was so popular, if she got in a fight with somebody, she had three more groupies who'd step in to comfort her. She had friends and boys.

When you came right down to it, all of my problems could be solved with more popularity.

I decided to go shopping soon and buy a new wardrobe. I'd get a complete makeover. I was going to be in—more in than Cami, and then she'd see I didn't need her friendship.

In biology, Mr. Parkinson gave us time to work on our projects. Frederick wrote the rough draft of our conclusion while I tried to figure out what to say for the hypothesis.

Hypothesis: If you cut the fins off a rocket, it will no longer fly right. We feel this is an important discovery and could affect other aspects of technology. For example, we also hypothesize that if you cut the wheels off a car, it will no longer run. Ditto for the handlebars of a bike. We are not sure why somebody would actually do any of this, but nonetheless, we wanted to prove it would be a bad idea.

Frederick looked over at my paper. "That's not our hypothesis. You haven't written anything about the center of gravity or the center of pressure."

"That's because I've forgotten what both of those things are."

Furthermore, we hypothesize that if you force two unalike people to become science partners, they will drive each other crazy before the assignment is due. This is especially true if one of them happens to be a bossy know-it-all.

"I've done my best to overlook your bossiness," Frederick told me.

"I was talking about you."

"I know you were talking about me. I was joking. Now quit goofing off and write the real hypothesis."

I crumpled up my paper and overhanded it into the wastebasket by the wall. A perfect shot. The next time Rochelle and Raleigh turned up their nose at basketball, I could point out the advantage of being able to stay in my seat while throwing wads of paper across the room to the garbage can. With this stupid hypothesis to write, it was a skill that would come in handy.

"It's the pits, isn't it?" Frederick said.

"My comprehension of science?"

"No, feeling like you're all alone in school." Frederick paused in his writing and leaned closer to me. "And by the way, I don't think standing up in English class and telling someone off really counts as poetry."

"I don't feel like I'm all alone in school," I said. I was trying to convince myself more than Frederick, but I did a lousy job of both.

Frederick shook his head at me. "You've barely looked at anyone all day, and you're not smiling."

"Sometimes I don't feel like smiling."

"I spent all last year acting the same way."

"You did?" I didn't remember Frederick not looking or smiling at anyone last year, but then, I didn't remember much about Frederick last year, beyond the time in math class when he gave everyone a blow-by-blow account of how he won the regional chess championship. Chess is slightly less exciting to watch than—say—sleeping cats, and even less fun to hear about. ▬▬

Frederick shrugged. "Finally I just got to the point where I stopped caring what other people thought about me. That makes everything easier. You still feel alone, but it doesn't bother you anymore."

I wasn't sure if that was a good motto or a really sad way to live life. I twirled my pencil between my fingers but couldn't write anything. "Look, Frederick, if I was ever a jerk to you last year, I'm sorry."

He went back to writing. "It's okay. If you were, I've been enough of a jerk to you this year to make up for it."

I wrote a sentence for a new hypothesis, decided it was no good, wadded the paper up, and chucked it into the wastepaper basket. Which was infinitely more fun than writing.

"You'll be okay," Frederick told me without looking up from his paper. "You're popular enough that you'll have a new best friend soon enough."

There was more to this statement than he said. He was unpopular, so he would continue to go through school feeling alone.

I wished I could do something about that. I wanted to change it for him somehow, but what could I do? He was a guy, and I was a girl, and if we started hanging around together, everyone would think we were going out. This was definitely not an "in" thing to do.

I tapped my pen against the next piece of notebook paper and felt worse than I had before.

Hypothesis: High school stinks.

Cami

The next few days went by slowly. Ethan avoided me when we were at our lockers, even though I told him again that I didn't have kleptomania. "In fact, I was vaccinated against it as a child, weren't you?"

"Probably," he said, and hurried off. I didn't even have time to tell him kleptomania isn't a disease, and there's no vaccination for it. Next time we were together at our lockers, I'd cough on him just to make him worry.

I ate lunch with Tisha and Barbara. Josie never talked to me. I never talked to her either, but somehow I always knew where she was in the hallway and the cafeteria. At first, people looked at me a lot during school. I could almost hear them recounting the story about our poetry fight in English. By the end of the week the staring had all pretty much stopped, except for Caroline, who made a habit of stationing herself in the hallway, staring at me, and then, when I noticed her, calling out, "See, you knew I was looking!"

She also did this in biology class to the point that I began to feel like one of those paranoid schizophrenics who think they're being watched all the time. Finally, to protect my sanity, I agreed that the sixth sense worked, that everything she believed was true, and promised once she became a psychic, I'd call her if I ever had delinquent pets that needed therapy— all so she'd stop staring at me.

For our next batch of research we met during lunch and sat at a table in the far corner. "Once it gets out that we're testing people's sixth sense, everyone will start checking to see if we're staring at them, and it won't be an accurate sampling anymore," she told me as she sipped Noni juice from a water bottle. "But we should be able to get some good data at first."

"Right." I figured once word got out that we were doing ESP research, people would indeed begin staring at us, but only because they thought we were strange. "Who should we stare at first?"

"How about Brendan? He's cute."

"No. He's sitting next to Ethan."

"But all the cute guys are sitting next to Ethan."

"Right, so let's stare at a girl instead."

Caroline sighed. "How about Erica?"

We stared at Erica while we ate our lunches. Fifty-two seconds later she looked over at us. Which just went to prove having a sixth sense must not be related to having a high IQ. Next we stared at Raleigh, or at least Caroline did; my gaze kept drifting over to Josie. Josie leaned over the table toward Rochelle, and the two talked as though they'd been friends forever.

I'd been replaced so easily. It was like I never meant anything to Josie to begin with.

Two minutes into our stare, Erica walked by our table. She was pretending to throw her lunch sack away in the garbage can by us, but there were garbage cans closer to her table, so I knew she'd come over to talk. She peered at our notebook. "What are you guys doing?"

"We're testing to see if people have psychic powers," Caroline said. "You scored pretty high. It took you less than a minute to realize we were staring at you."

"It's our science fair project," I added.

She cocked her head at me. "You must score pretty low on the ESP, Cami. Otherwise you would have known Ethan was only paying attention to you to make Ashley jealous."

I gripped my pencil, not letting any emotion show on my face. "Oh, really?"

"Yeah. Ashley broke up with Ethan to go out with Jeff. Ethan was just getting back at her by talking to you. Now Ashley's broken up with Jeff, and she and Ethan are back together."

She turned and left before I could say anything, which was just as well, since I couldn't think of anything to say. What do you say when someone tells you that the guy you liked—the guy you fought with your best friend over—was just using you? Was she right? Or was that just what Ashley wanted to believe? Somehow, at that moment it didn't matter. The result was still the same. Ashley and Ethan were back together, and Josie and I hadn't spoken in a week.

Caroline put one hand over her temple and closed her eyes. "I'm getting a reading on Erica's future." She hummed for a moment, as though she were a dial tone. "Years from now she and Ashley both join the cast of a reality show, where they are forced to eat rodents for prize money. Sadly, neither of them win, and they go to live in Hollywood, working as waitresses while they wait for their big break. That doesn't happen either."

"I'd be happy to give them both a few breaks."

"As for Ethan, he becomes a genetic biologist working on ways to make bigger chickens for KFC. He succeeds, but during a freak accident he's attacked by a flock of three-foot-tall roosters and is forced into taking an early retirement. He recovers eventually, but gets a nervous twitch every time he hears anything that resembles pecking."

Despite feeling lousy, I cracked a smile. "You know, I think you may have psychic powers after all."

Caroline's eyes fluttered open, looking at me sympathetically. "Ethan is a jerk. Who'd want to go out with a guy who just uses people like that?"

"Right."

"You're better off without him."

"Right."

And I was also better off without friends who lied about me at the first moment that things didn't go their way. Only I didn't feel better off about either of those things.

The only thing that was better was this: for the first time I realized Caroline was not such a bad science partner after all.

Josie

During our game on Friday, Cami hardly passed me the ball, so I hardly passed the ball to her, and of course Ashley and Erica didn't want to pass it to either of us. Instead of a team, we looked like five girls on the court who just happened to be wearing the same outfits. We lost by twelve points. I was still the high scorer of the game, so I didn't feel it was a total loss. I was going to play with Rebecca Lobo. So there.

After the game, as my parents and I were leaving, we walked by Cami and her parents. Our mothers said an awkward hello to each other, sadness in their voices. I wondered what Cami's parents thought of me now.

Driving home in the car, my parents were silent. I sat in the backseat, darkness around me, listening to the hum of the tires against the street. Dad glanced at me over his shoulder. "How do you feel about the way you played tonight?"

"We lost," I said, as though that should explain everything.

"Why do you think you lost?" Dad said.

I shrugged. "You win some, you lose some."

"You win more if you pass the ball," Mom said. "Don't you think it's time for you to forgive Cami?"

"I can't trust her anymore."

"Trust and forgiveness are two different things."

"But she—"

"Forgiveness isn't about what Cami did," Mom cut me off. "It's about what you're going to do. You forgive for you—so you can let go of the anger inside of you and get on with your life. Tonight's game is proof of what happens when you hold a grudge. You keep hold of that ball, and you all lose."

I didn't answer. I knew Mom had a point, but it wasn't that easy. I couldn't just decide, Hey, I'm not mad at Cami anymore—none of the stuff she did hurts anymore.

It did hurt.

At school on Monday, I saw Ethan and Ashley walking down the hallway hand in hand, which meant he hadn't asked Cami to go out with him after all. I felt happy about this for thirty seconds, and then felt really awful. I had just meant to get back at Cami with the kleptomaniac story, not ruin everything for her. Had he actually believed me over Cami, or was it the yelling-poems-at-each-other in English that undid the romance?

Either way, seeing Ashley and Ethan together was living, physical proof I'd hurt Cami too.

On the way out of biology class I caught up with Ethan as he walked down the hallway. I had barely looked at Ethan, let alone spoken to him, since the poem-reading incident. It was embarrassing to even be in the same room with him now that the whole school knew Cami and I had fought over him.

But I had to talk to him to clear my conscience. He took long strides, and I hurried beside him, clutching my books while I tried to figure out the best way to start a conversation.

There wasn't a good way, so I just blurted out, "Hey, Ethan, do you remember when I told you about Cami having kleptomania? You knew I was just pulling your leg, right? Cami doesn't really have it, just like your shirt wasn't really on backward that day. I was just joking around."

Ethan only glanced at me as we walked. "Right. I knew you were joking."

"Good, because I wouldn't want you to think less of Cami because of what I said about her."

He shrugged his shoulder. "What does it matter what I think of Cami? Does she still have a thing for me or something?" The question was not so bad in and of itself, but the way he said it—with a sort of half sneer—made me catch my breath.

"I don't know what she thinks of you," I said. "I just thought you ought to know the truth."

His chin tilted down at me condescendingly. "I'm going out with Ashley now, and I don't think I should be talking to you about Cami." He veered away from me, and I stopped altogether, standing in the hallway while a flow of students walked around me.

Ethan had not only dismissed Cami, he'd dismissed me too. All of the time I had spent dreaming of him—and he considered me an annoyance, someone not even worth the effort of politeness.

I know you're going out with Ashley, I wanted to call after him, and you deserve each other.

Frederick called me after practice, wanting to know when we could get together to work on our poster board. Everyone else would be putting their boards together on the day they were due, but not us. Frederick wanted to finish our board as soon as possible, probably so he could bug me about revisions until March, when we had the science fair.

I invited Frederick to come over to my house—making sure Sadie and Kristen took Jack to the park. I was not about to have them hovering around, giggling that a boy had come to see me. I also asked my mother not to do anything to embarrass me.

"Embarrass you?" she asked. "What do I ever do to embarrass you?"

Which is one of those questions parents use to trick you into saying something that will get you grounded.

"Just don't come in while we're in the kitchen, okay?"

Mom threw up her hands. "You turn fourteen, and suddenly you don't want parents. Fine. I'll tell everyone you came to earth on a comet, like Superman."

But when Frederick arrived, she said hello, then left us alone to work.

We set everything up on the kitchen table, spreading out our graphs and pictures while we figured out how to arrange things on the poster board. Frederick changed the wording of every single thing I'd written about the project. I didn't mind. I wasn't sure how to use the words *computational fluid dynamics* in a sentence correctly anyway. We painted the poster board blue with white clouds and then taped our findings, trajectory plots, and rocket pictures onto it. We fought over the lettering of the title. He just wanted to write ROCKET STABILITY in marker, and I insisted on using stencils and glitter glue.

"Why do girls have to make everything pretty?" he asked as I traced the letters in gold. "It's about rockets. It's not supposed to be pretty."

"It looks better this way."

He stood over the poster board and sighed. "My science project glitters."

"Should I put some golden stars in the background to tie the whole look together?"

"No. You're not putting glitter stars on my science project."

"It's my science project too." I leaned over the table and put stars around our hypothesis and our conclusion. "I'll make one of them a shooting star."

Frederick held out his hand to me. "Give me the glue. You're getting carried away."

"It looks good."

"I'm taking the board home with me. Otherwise you'll paint in sunsets and sprinkle perfume on the thing while I'm gone."

"You're so paranoid." I handed him the glue. "Although a couple of Scottish terriers in the bottom corner would be cute."

"Give me the board. I'm taking it home right now."

I slapped his hands away. "If you touch it now, you'll smear the stars. Then the judges will wonder why we have a bunch of golden blobs on our poster board, and I'll be forced to make up some story about UFOs."

He put both hands in front of him on the table and glared at me. "You're not going to say the word *UFO* when talking about my science project to the judges. In fact, don't say anything at all. Pretend you're mute." He sighed, then covered his face with one hand. "I'd forgotten, the judges will ask you questions too. You'll ruin everything."

"Your confidence in me is so touching."

"Okay, I'm *confident* you'll ruin everything."

If anyone else had said this stuff to me, I would have either burst out in tears or slapped him. Maybe both. But I'd gotten used to Frederick, and it just seemed funny to see him so panicked. I blew on one of the stars to help it dry. "I'll tell the judges next year we're doing a project on fingernail polish."

"No, we're not. Next year I'm doing one on global positioning satellite signals, and if you want to be my partner, you won't be decorating our poster board with any more glitter stars."

Which was not what I thought he'd say. I expected him to say he was never being my partner again, and the fact that he hadn't seemed almost like a compliment. Suddenly, there in the kitchen, it didn't seem to matter so much what the kids at school would think about Frederick and me hanging out together. Why should I let everyone else determine who my friends were? I leaned over and blew on the stars again. "You realize I don't know anything about global-positioning-whatever-you-said."

"Yeah, I figured as much."

"Any chance you'll be chased out of someone's yard by angry dogs during it?"

He waved a hand over the poster board. "How long does this take to dry?"

"A long time. Come on, let's go play basketball while we're waiting."

Frederick straightened up and huffed. "I don't play basketball."

"You do now. And while I'm teaching you how to shoot, we'll work on your people skills."

I pushed away from the table and walked to the kitchen door. He stood up and followed me reluctantly. "I don't want to work on my people skills."

"Which is part of the problem," I said. "We'll work on your bad attitude first."

He huffed again, but then he smiled.

Twelve

Cami

We played Thatcher and lost the game. Again. And got yelled at by Coach Melbourne for not passing enough. Again. She put in a lot of time yelling at us at practice, which may come in handy if she ever decides to quit coaching basketball and become a drill sergeant.

I've decided Josie has taken our fight worse than I thought. She's started talking to Frederick at school, even when she doesn't have to. She is obviously suffering from some sort of identity crisis—either that or she thinks I really do have kleptomania, and she's trying to tempt me into stealing Frederick away from her. Like I would fall for that.

Josie

Cami has taken our fight worse than I thought. She's started hanging around with Caroline, Madame Pet Psychic. Cami is either having some sort of nervous breakdown or she suspects her cat has feline depression. It's hard to tell with cats, since they sleep all day anyway.

Frederick and I have become better friends. We IM each other a lot, and he helps me with my homework if I need it. At first I was worried he would want to be more than friends, but it turns out he has a thing for Jessica Bing, who is one of those petite, perky girls on the cheerleading squad. Frederick and a cheerleader. And to think of the grief he's given me about being a jockette.

Anyway, I sent him a card before he went to his regional chess tournament. When he got back, he called me right off to tell me he'd come in second—beaten by Daniel the Knight Slayer. Frederick still got to go to the state tournament, so he didn't mind that much. He went on and on about the competition. I think he was just happy to have someone to tell about it, and I was happy to listen.

Cami

During our fourth game against Benson, the team still wasn't passing to one another enough, and at halftime we were down by ten points. Coach Melbourne hauled us all into the locker room to scream at us.

"What happened to teamwork? You guys are overlooking people who are wide open and going for impossible shots. Don't you care about winning? Don't you want to hold your heads high when you walk out of here tonight? I'm ashamed of the way some of you have been playing." She held out her finger, shaking it at all of us. "And I'll tell you another thing, if you think I'll let any one of you play with Rebecca Lobo when you haven't been passing the ball to your teammates, you're dead wrong. MVP does not stand for Most Vanity Points. The MVP will be the most valuable player *to the team*, the girl whose performance makes the biggest difference to *everyone* on the court—and that includes rebounds, assists, communication, and leadership. Stop playing for yourselves and play for your team. Do you understand me?"

We all mumbled we did.

During the second half the whole team passed to each other like crazy. We narrowed Benson's lead, tied, and then lost in overtime.

I hated losing. I also hated that Josie was still the high scorer, with Ashley close behind.

I was in third place again. When I said I was done being number two, this was not what I had in mind.

Still, I hoped Coach Melbourne at least noticed the fact that I'd been passing the ball. I had the most assists of anyone on the team.

Only Mom came to this game because Benson was so far away. As we walked across the parking lot, she draped her arm across my shoulders. "You played well."

"Not as well as Josie."

"I thought you were playing against the other team, not against Josie."

I rolled my eyes at her. We reached our car, and Mom got behind the wheel while I climbed in the passenger side. "It isn't fair. I work harder, and she's still better."

Mom took her keys from her purse, inserted one into the ignition, and then pulled her seat belt across her lap. "If you concentrate on what you don't have, you'll never be happy."

"I don't want to be happy. I want to be better than Josie."

Mom shook her head at me while she edged the car out of the parking space. "And that sums up your problem."

Well, maybe, but that didn't tell me how to fix it. I was jealous and bitter, but I didn't *want* to feel that way. How do you make yourself not feel something when you already feel it?

I pulled my own seat belt on. "She never even said she was sorry."

"You can't rewrite the past, Cami. You can only write your future. Do you want to go through your whole future feeling angry about this?"

I didn't see that I really had a choice.

Josie

Coach Melbourne likes Cami better than me. They both think basketball is war, so they have more in common.

As our team left the court after the ending buzzer, Cami wiped tears away from her cheeks. In the locker room, Coach Melbourne put her arm around Cami and gave her a private pep talk. Probably reviewing battle plans. *We'll head off the enemy next time. Keep your chin up, soldier.*

I wonder if anyone who plays professional ball feels like I do about the game—that it's just a game—or whether all of them approach the sport like soldiers, ready to give their lives for the battle.

I'd like to ask Rebecca Lobo about this. Is basketball still fun in the WNBA, or does every lost game feel like a personal failure?

I've never cried after a basketball game, or—as I've seen some girls do—in the middle.

I don't want a job that involves crying on a regular basis.

The next day after practice, Coach Melbourne sat us all down and told us there had been a change of plans. Instead of Rebecca coming to one of our home games, she was inviting us to play an invitational game in Chandler with the Basha Bears.

"It will create more media coverage of the event," Coach Melbourne told us, "because it's easy to send a news van to Chandler, but Rebecca was having a hard time convincing the press to make a trip to Sanchez. Plus the Bears will charge a small fee for people to see the game and then donate the proceeds to programs that help underprivileged kids play sports."

Coach Melbourne said all of this in a cheerful, upbeat voice to let us know it was really a good thing, although I knew our parents were not likely to see a three-hour trip to Chandler and a door charge in the same light.

She picked up a stack of white papers and handed them to Ashley, who was sitting down in front of her. "Everyone's parents will need to fill out a parental permission slip for the trip. I want these back as soon as possible."

I folded my paper but didn't put it in my backpack. I wanted to hold on to it and read it over a few more times.

Suddenly, with this piece of paper in my hands, Rebecca Lobo seemed very near. This was no longer something we were just talking about, this was something we were actually going to do.

I looked around at the other girls, all picking up their things, white papers fluttering as they headed to the door. Cami put her permission slip into the front section of her backpack, away from the rest of her books so it wouldn't get crumpled.

She'd probably be the first to turn in her slip. She'd most likely have her mom sign it in the parking lot and run it back in to Coach Melbourne.

Well, two could play that game. I'd have my mom sign my slip right now too. And if it would help me win most valuable player, I could even force a few tears after the next game. This was one time when basketball really was war.

Cami

I counted down the days, the hours, and then the minutes until Saturday, when Mom took me to the parking lot for our trip to Chandler. We were supposed to meet at 3:15. I made Mom drop me off at 3:00 because Coach Melbourne had given us a big lecture about how she was tired of people showing up late for away games, and she was instituting a zero-tolerance waiting policy. If you didn't show up on time, you didn't come. I was the first player there, but I didn't mind. I wanted Coach Melbourne to see that not only was I a dedicated player, I was punctual.

I went and stood by Coach Melbourne as she talked to the assistant coaches. At 3:10 the other girls began to arrive. Ashley and Erica came together and waited, leaning up against the hood of the Holts' car. Josie still hadn't shown up.

Coach Melbourne had told us at practice that we'd pull out of the parking lot at 3:30, but the bus was nowhere around. At 3:25 she called the transportation director on her mobile phone.

Josie still hadn't come. I didn't think Coach Melbourne would really leave any of the players behind, especially the best player on the team, but if Josie held all of us up, well, good-bye to Josie's chance of being chosen to play with Rebecca.

Three-thirty came. The bus didn't.

At 3:35 Mrs. Caraway drove into the parking lot and dropped Josie off. She carried her duffel bag in one hand and a large Rubbermaid container in the other. She must have been one of those who signed up for making cookies for the bus trip. They were probably Mrs. Caraway's famous double chocolate chip cookies—a blatant attempt to buy Coach Melbourne's favors. I wished I'd thought of that. I wished my mother could bake.

Mrs. Caraway waved good-bye, called out of the window, "We'll see you at the game!" and drove off. Coach Melbourne was so busy yelling at people on her mobile phone, she didn't even notice Josie had come after the deadline. Apparently not only balls but buses preferred Josie.

At 3:40 Coach Melbourne told us the bus had broken down, but they were sending another one over. At 3:55 the coach was back on her mobile phone, yelling at people from the transportation department because a bus still hadn't shown up.

Ashley's mom, Mrs. Holt, who was one of the parents waiting around in the parking lot to see us off, walked up to the coach. "The girls are missing out on their warm-up time. Why don't we just put them in cars and drive them up? Between the parents and the assistant coaches, we have enough cars here, and the parents will need to leave soon anyway if we want to get good seats."

Coach Melbourne let out a sigh, scanned the parking lot as though she might spot a bus tucked away somewhere if she looked hard enough, then nodded. "We don't want the girls to have to forfeit the game because they're late. Let's load everyone up and make sure we stick together, caravan-style. I don't want anyone lost in Chandler somewhere." Coach Melbourne let out one of her ear-piercing whistles and waved everyone to come over. "Change of plans. We're going in cars, and I want you all to listen up so we don't waste any more time." She turned to Ashley's mom. "How many girls can you take?"

"Four," Mrs. Holt said.

"Okay. Ashley, Erica, Cami, and Josie—you ride in the Holts' car."

Coach Melbourne then went on to list the other girls and where they would ride. I picked up my duffel bag and wandered over to the Holts' green Honda. Was Coach Melbourne mean or just clueless? Why in the world would she assign me to ride with the three people on the team who didn't like me?

Mrs. Holt opened up the trunk of her Honda, and I dropped my duffel bag into it. Then, without looking at any of the other girls, I climbed into the front seat. It was going to be one long, awkward drive.

Josie

Ashley and Erica sat beside me in the backseat, talking to each other and ignoring me. Cami sat in the front seat beside Mrs. Holt and also ignored me. And I was going to have to endure three hours of this. I wished I had brought a book. I wished I'd brought anything. Doing homework would have been preferable to staring out the car window at the expanse of dirt and sagebrush that spread out along the highway.

At first I'd felt lucky the bus was late. I'd been ready on time, but the cookies took longer to make than normal—probably because Jack tried to help and ended up tipping the first batch on the floor. The second batch didn't get out of the oven until 3:15. Then when we went to put them in a container, they were so hot they kept falling apart. I stood in the kitchen blowing on the cookie sheet until I was about to hyperventilate, while my mom waved an oven mitt over them, chanting, "Coach Melbourne won't really leave you. You're the star player."

I was so relieved when I pulled into the parking lot and found out the bus was late and Coach Melbourne wasn't enforcing her zero-tolerance waiting policy, but now I was stuck in a car with three people who were ignoring me, and I had no idea where my cookies were. I'd given them to Coach Melbourne as soon as she'd gotten off her mobile phone.

The road stretched out in a straight black line that cut through the land. I counted the seconds between the road mile signs. Whichever car had my cookies would probably eat them all, and I'd be starving by the time we reached Chandler.

I watched the spindly sagebrush and occasional cactus or ocotillo flash by the car. I checked the clock on the dashboard to see if the number really changed once a minute. It did.

Ashley and Erica talked about guys at school. They started out with Ethan. Ashley said in this patronizing voice that I knew was directed toward Cami or me, or maybe both of us, that she was thinking of breaking up with Ethan again because he was just too immature. She needed someone who acted like a man, not like a juvenile.

Right. Good luck finding one of those in the high school.

She continued with this topic for a few more minutes, I suppose to rub it in our faces that neither of us could get what she could casually throw away.

I wondered if Ethan knew how Ashley talked about him behind his back. It seemed pathetic that she had so little loyalty to him, and even more pathetic that Ethan put up with her. I mean, really, was it so important to have a gorgeous girlfriend that he was willing to completely overlook her personality?

Ashley and Erica next talked about Pete and Ted, only there wasn't a Pete or Ted at school, so either they were using code names for other guys or they'd completely lost their grip on reality and were now making up boyfriends.

Cami kept drumming her fingers against the armrest. She was probably busy making mental lists: Ten ways in which I can win over Ethan again. Five things I can do to flatter Coach Melbourne before she chooses who will play with Rebecca Lobo. One hundred excuses why nothing is ever my fault.

An hour and a half after we started, our car caravan turned off Interstate 8 at Gila Bend to buy gas and let people use the bathroom. Ashley and Erica got money from Ashley's mom and went inside the Chevron station to buy snacks. Cami stayed in her seat. Apparently she hadn't brought money with her either. I wondered if Ashley and Erica planned on sharing with us or whether we'd be stuck watching them eat potato chips just like we were stuck listening to them talk about how Pete and Ted were *so funny* and just said the *cutest things*.

Mrs. Holt filled up the car, washed the windshield, and then disappeared inside the gas station. Cami and I sat alone in the car.

I watched kids from the other cars going in and out of the gas station. Lucy Simmons was eating one of my cookies. At least I knew which car they were in. Ashley bounced up to the Honda carrying sodas and a bag of Doritos. "Coach says she wants everyone to use the restrooms here so we don't have to stop again until we get to Chandler."

"I don't need to use the bathroom," I said.

Ashley shrugged and slid into the car. "Fine. You don't have to do what the coach says if you don't want to. It's not like I'll tell her you blew her off." She ripped open the bag of chips and popped one into her mouth. "Your secret is safe with me."

I opened the car door and got out. Cami got out of the passenger side at the same time.

Lucy saw me emerging from the Holts' car and waved. "Hey, great cookies, Josie. I could live on these."

"Thanks. Save me one."

She popped the last of the cookie into her mouth. "They're going fast. You'd better come to our car and get one if you want one."

"After I'm done in the bathroom," I called to her.

Lucy walked back to her car, and Cami and I crossed the parking lot in silence. Cami loved my mom's cookies, but I knew she'd never bring herself to ask for one.

The restroom was around the side of the gas station, and as we walked to it we met Erica coming the other way. She carried a key attached to a large plastic triangle that read WOMEN.

"Are you guys going to use the bathroom?" She handed me the key without waiting for our answer. "Mikala is in there right now. I was just returning the key for her, so don't walk in on her. She might be awhile still. You know how long she takes."

I didn't. I'd never timed Mikala in the bathroom, but I nodded at Erica anyway.

Cami and I walked around the corner of the gas station and went and stood by the door. It was painted white but had dirty brown streaks across it and gray smudges around the handle.

I hated gas station restrooms.

We both stood and watched the door. I fingered the plastic rectangle and wondered how many people before me had touched this key chain and whether or not you could catch diseases that way. A minute went by. Then another. Apparently Erica was right about Mikala and the bathroom. The silence between Cami and I felt tense, like when you watch someone blow a balloon bigger and bigger and you know any moment it will pop.

I wanted to say something just so we had something to do besides staring at the closed door. "So how's your science project coming along?" I asked. "Find anyone with psychic powers?"

Cami gave me a cold look, which I thought was totally uncalled-for, since that *was* her science project. "Things are fine. How about you? You seem to be getting along really well with Frederick at school."

She said this nicely, but I knew it was an insult. I smiled back at her anyway. "Frederick takes some getting used to, but he's okay. He's the type of person that says whatever is on his mind, which isn't always kind, but at least you know he's always being honest with you."

Cami's eyes narrowed. "Yeah. I can tell how much honesty means to you, since you were so honest with Ethan about me."

"Just like you were so honest with me about Ethan."

"I never lied to you about Ethan. I just—" Cami's voice broke off, and she looked out across the grass embankment that separated the gas station from the road. "Isn't that the Holts' car leaving?"

I turned and watched a green Honda turn onto the road that left the gas station. The car headed toward the highway.

"She wouldn't have left us. There must have been another Honda like the Holts' in the parking lot."

Cami took a step toward the embankment. "I think that's Lucy's mom's car following them."

I knocked on the bathroom door. "Come on, Mikala. We have to leave."

No answer.

We both watched as a stream of cars passed by on the road.

"They wouldn't have left the three of us. Someone would notice we were missing." I knocked on the door again. Still no answer.

Cami pointed up at the street. "Look, there goes Coach Melbourne's pickup, and she said she wanted to be the last one in the caravan."

There was no mistaking Coach Melbourne's cherry red Silverado or the Connecticut Sun sticker on the back of her truck. She *had* left.

We stood there dumbstruck while the Silverado zoomed across the road and disappeared out of view.

"You know," I said, "I think Coach Melbourne has taken that zero-tolerance waiting policy way too far."

Cami grabbed the key from me and inserted it into the bathroom lock. She turned the key and swung open the door. The bathroom was empty. Mikala had never been inside.

Cami let out an angry grunt. "Erica tricked us. She set us up to be left behind!"

"No, Mrs. Holt wouldn't have gone without us." For one

second we looked at each other, and then both took off at a sprint around the gas station to the parking lot.

No green Honda. I didn't recognize any of the cars that were filling up.

Cami turned around, hands on her hips, panting. "I can't believe this. They really left us."

"Mrs. Holt will notice we're not in the car. She'll come back for us. Any moment we'll see her car rolling down the road in this direction." We both stood in the parking lot, staring at the empty road. A red compact drove by, then a white minivan. I didn't give up hope. "She'll feel so bad about leaving us, maybe she'll even make Ashley share her Doritos with us."

Cami turned and walked back to the curb in front of the gas station entrance. She sat down, elbows on her knees and chin in her hands, and watched the road.

I stayed on my feet, but I walked over to where Cami sat. It was pointless to sit down when any second Mrs. Holt would pull back into the parking lot. "And just think of all the great comebacks you'll have for Ashley the next time she bothers you—'Hey, Ashley, you may think my mother's ugly, but at least she's smart enough to tell when the car is half empty.'"

Cami didn't smile. "You're right. No one is that stupid. She left us on purpose."

"Mrs. Holt wouldn't leave us on purpose."

"You know, for someone who's in all honors classes, you don't get it, do you? She left us because she's Ashley's mom, and she wants Ashley to be chosen to play with Rebecca Lobo."

The idea made my chest constrict like I'd been hit. Still, I couldn't believe it. "Mrs. Holt is not going to show up in Chandler without us. I mean, it's not like Coach Melbourne won't notice we're missing."

Cami kicked at the pavement with one shoe. "The coach will notice, but by then it will be too late. It'll be an hour-and-a-half trip back here to pick us up and another hour and a half to get us to Chandler. We'll miss halftime."

"But Mrs. Holt will get in so much trouble."

"She'll have some good excuse. She wouldn't have left us without a good excuse planned out."

"There aren't any good excuses. She'll come back."

We waited for five minutes. A few cars pulled into the gas station, but no one we knew. "We should call someone," I said.

Cami glanced at her watch. "My family is already on their way to Chandler. Isn't yours?"

"Even Kevin? Isn't he at home?"

"He went skiing with a friend's family in Flagstaff this weekend."

I kept my gaze on the street. "What about your parent's mobile phone? Can't you call and have them pick us up?"

She shook her head. "They gave me the phone in case I needed to call before they left. It's in my duffel bag in the Holts' trunk."

I sunk down on the curb beside Cami. She didn't even bother to ask if my parents had a mobile phone. She knew they didn't. My mom thought they were too expensive, and my dad thought they were a nuisance.

"We've got to do something," I said. "We can't just sit here and let Ashley steal Rebecca Lobo."

"Steal her from you, you mean. You're the high scorer." Cami shook her head; her words came out sharp and biting. "Ashley probably didn't even mean to leave me behind. I just got unlucky because I was riding with you."

"Yeah, too bad you weren't riding with Madame Pet Psychic. She could have predicted the bathroom was empty, and then asked all the birds here at the gas station to help rescue you from your plight. Right now a flock of pigeons could be spelling out 'go back' on Coach Melbourne's windshield."

Cami tilted her chin down, her eyes angry slits. "And it's too bad you weren't riding with Frederick. He's so annoying, Ashley and Erica would have both willingly stranded *themselves* here at the gas station just so they didn't have to ride with him all the way to Chandler."

"You don't know anything about Frederick, so you should just be quiet."

"And you don't know anything about Caroline, so you should just be quiet."

We stared at each other, neither one of us turning away from the other's gaze. Seconds went by. My heart beat as fast as it did after running laps. "So do you want to just sit and yell at each other, or do you want to think of some way out of here?"

For a moment she hesitated, like she did just want to sit here and yell at me, but then said, "Let's think of a way out of here."

Thirteen

Cami

The gas station attendant, a man whose arm tattoos were probably older than Josie and I put together, let us use the phone at the counter after we'd brought back the bathroom key to him. His scraggly gray hair was pulled back in a ponytail, although this was probably not a fashion statement, but an indication the guy was too lazy to get a haircut. His shirt didn't look like it had been washed in weeks. While Josie dialed directory assistance to see if they could give her Coach Melbourne's mobile phone number—they couldn't, mobile phone numbers aren't in the database—he watched us suspiciously, like he expected us to suddenly break into the hot dog machine.

I called my mobile phone, just in case someone could hear it over Ashley and Erica's conversation about Ted and Pete, but no one answered.

Then we took turns calling everyone we could think of back in Sanchez in an attempt to find someone who knew Coach Melbourne's number.

Hardly anyone was home. Either more people from Sanchez were heading up to Chandler than I'd imagined, or no one stayed at home on Saturday afternoons.

Finally Josie got a hold of Frederick. She explained the situation to him, then paused, leaning up against the check-out counter. "Stop laughing, Frederick, it isn't funny. Can you call some teachers from school and see if somebody has Coach Melbourne's mobile phone number?"

Another pause. "I don't know who. I thought you were on a first-name basis with all the teachers. You probably have a few of them on your speed dial. One of them must have her mobile phone number." A pause in which Josie tapped her fingers against the countertop. "Just try to find it. Try anything."

Josie gave Frederick the phone number of the gas station, then hung up.

Next Josie called the police. I was hoping they'd volunteer to drive us to Chandler. After all, they were public servants, and we were the public and in need of serving, but the officer said all they could do was send someone over to Basha High and let Coach Melbourne know they'd left two students at the Gila Bend Chevron.

As if she wouldn't figure that out herself when we didn't climb out of Mrs. Holt's car. I suggested loudly that the police should arrest Mrs. Holt, since leaving people at a gas station when they should be playing with Rebecca Lobo is obviously a criminal offense, but Josie just glared at me, and I don't think the police took my suggestion to heart.

Then we stood staring at the phone, waiting for someone to call us back. Waiting for a better idea.

"We could hitchhike," Josie said.

"Yeah, and then we could be kidnapped and never seen again. We're not hitchhiking."

We went back to staring at the phone.

I turned toward the gas station guy. He was still watching us, but it might not have been just because he was creepy. We were probably the most interesting thing that had happened in this gas station in a long time. "Are there any taxicabs in Gila Bend?" I asked.

"There's Bert's Towing and Discount Cab. But it's a long drive to Chandler. You might have to pay him extra to go all the way out there."

"We don't have any money," Josie said.

I grabbed the phone book from the counter and flipped through the Bs until I found the number. "We can have our parents pay the cabdriver once we get to Chandler." My hands shook as I dialed the phone. I was so excited to have thought of the idea, and at the same time nervous it wouldn't work.

Bert himself answered the phone. I explained the situation to him and asked if he could pick us up right away.

"But you don't have any money?" he asked skeptically. "Do you realize what cab fare runs? It's a dollar fifty a mile, and you're talking about driving upward of seventy miles. That'll run you over a hundred dollars without the tip. What if I drive you all the way to Chandler and your parents don't want to pay?"

I knew already our parents wouldn't want to pay—especially Josie's—but they would. This was an emergency.

"They'll pay you," I said. "I'm their only daughter, and they love me."

"I'll tell you what," Bert drawled into the phone, "you get half the money up front, and I'll let your parents pay the other half when I take you to Chandler."

"But we don't have any money," I repeated.

"Then sell your Walkmans and Gameboys. You teenagers always have those."

"I don't—"

But he didn't let me finish. "I can't sit here and talk with you on the phone all day. I've got business to take care of. You call me if you get the money."

Then Bert hung up.

I slammed the phone back down on the receiver, which earned me a dirty look from the creepy gas station guy. "Bert wants us to have half the fare—fifty dollars before he'll take us."

Josie's mouth hung open. "He's charging us a hundred dollars just to take us to Chandler? We could rent two cars for that price."

"Except neither of us is old enough to drive." I smiled over at the creepy gas station guy. "Could you lend us fifty dollars? Our parents will pay you when we drive back to Sanchez."

"Mrs. Holt will pay you back," Josie said. "She's the one who left us."

The creepy gas station guy just folded his arms and snorted, which I assumed meant, "No way."

Josie leaned up against the counter and lifted her hands in frustration. "Then we're stuck here waiting."

Which meant neither of us would play with Rebecca.

At least that prevented me from having to see Josie be the

chosen one, once again. I could tell myself as I stood here waiting next to the boxes of Cheez-Its and snow globes of melted Arizona snowmen that Coach Melbourne would have chosen me. I could tell myself I wasn't number two.

I looked from Josie to the dirty floors and shelves of candy bars, to the rack of postcards showing cactus and jack-a-lopes.

We couldn't stand here for hours. Not while Rebecca Lobo was waiting for us. I was too close to my dream to have it taken away from me now.

I picked up a pen from the counter, took Josie's arm, and pulled her toward the door. "Come on. We're not waiting." Just before I pushed the front door open, I called back to the creepy gas station guy, "We're going out in the parking lot for a few minutes. If any calls come in for us, please let us know, all right?"

He grunted, which I assumed meant, "I don't get paid to be your receptionist," but I hoped he'd tell us anyway.

We went outside and stopped in front of the garbage can. I gingerly sifted through paper towels, candy bar wrappers, and used cups.

At last I pulled out an empty granola bar box. Josie watched me with eyebrows raised. "So what's your idea, and why does it involve trash?"

I ripped the box and turned it over so I had a blank piece of cardboard. "We'll make a sign, explaining that we're stranded and need cab fare, then we'll go stand by the parking lot entrance so people can give us money as they drive by."

"Sort of like those WILL WORK FOR FOOD signs?" Josie asked.

"Right."

"Except we're not offering to do jobs, we just want people to give us money for nothing?"

"Right."

"I don't think that will work."

I swatted her arm with the cardboard. "I know it's degrading to beg, but I'm trying to get us to Chandler. Do you have any better ideas?"

She sighed, took a deep breath, then prodded through the garbage can. She pulled out a used Slurpee cup and shook the last of its contents back into the trash. With the cup outstretched in her hand, she turned to me. "We'll sing."

"Sing?"

"A lot of beginning performers get their start that way. They sing on street corners and in restaurants, and people drop money in their cups."

I glanced at the people at the pumps. A haggard mother wiped off her windshield while two children inside the car made faces at each other. At another pump, a man in a cowboy hat and frayed jeans filled up his truck while he took chewing tobacco from his pocket. At the next pump a balding man of about seventy fiddled with his gas cap. "Yeah, but this is a gas station, neither one of us can sing, and no one will want to touch that used Slurpee cup, let alone put money in it."

"If we're singing, we can walk up to people. It'll be faster than just hoping people feel charitable as they drive by us." Josie stepped off the curb and walked toward the pumps. "How about one of Celine Dion's songs? People love those."

I followed her, taking halting half steps and wondering if it was legal to pester people for money while they filled up their cars. Standing by the side of the road holding a sign and looking forlorn would have been so much less pushy. "Josie, we've lost our rides, and we've lost a lot of time, do we need to lose all our dignity too?"

She ignored me and walked up to the older man. He'd just inserted the gas nozzle into his car. "Hello, sir, would you care for some music while you're filling up? We're trying to earn money for cab fare." She cleared her throat and belted out—off key—the beginning of "My Heart Will Go On." "Every night in my dreams, I see you, I feel you . . ."

Her singing didn't improve as she went along.

I put my hand over my face but could still see the man looking at us, then behind him, then to either side, to see if Josie was actually singing to him. She increased her volume and held out the Slurpee cup to him. "You have come to sho-ow you go oo-on!"

He took a step closer to the pump and put his hand back on the nozzle, as though to hurry it along.

"Join me for the chorus, Cami!" she sung out.

My own voice was quieter, wavering, and no more on key than Josie's. "Near far, wherever we are—I mean, you are. Oh, it doesn't matter. It's something about the heart, and the heart must go oo-on."

I gave up on the words then and started humming. Josie stepped toward the man, still holding out the Slurpee cup. "You'll always be in our hearts, sir, if you help us get cab fare."

His eyes took on a trapped expression, as though next

we'd be asking for his car keys. He thrust his hand in his pockets and emptied its contents into the Slurpee cup. Then he chucked the gas nozzle back on the pump, climbed into his car, and peeled out of the parking lot while Josie waved and called, "God bless you!" after him.

I took the cup from her and dumped the contents into my hand.

Josie leaned over me to see our stash. "What did he give us?"

"Two quarters, two dimes, three pennies, nail clippers, and half a roll of Certs. He probably didn't mean to give us those last two things." I dropped the nail clippers back into the cup because it was gross touching some old guy's nail clippers.

Josie put her hands on her hips. "Seventy-three cents? Do you realize how long it will take us to get cab fare at this rate?"

I poured the money back into the cup. "Well, I'll tell you one thing. The only tip Bert is getting from us is the nail clippers and the Certs."

Josie held out her hand. "Nope, I'm starving. I want the Certs. Bert just gets the nail clippers."

I handed her the Certs and broke out laughing. I couldn't help myself. Suddenly it all seemed so funny—the two of us chasing away gas station customers with Celine Dion songs. Josie unrolled the Certs wrapper, the smile growing on her face until she was laughing too. "This is the worst day of my life since I fell down the up escalator at the mall."

"And the day is only half over," I said. "We still have

forty-nine dollars and twenty-seven cents left to earn." I leaned up against the gas pump, and Josie laughed so hard she nearly spit out her Certs.

"Maybe if one of us pretends to have a seizure, an ambulance will take us into a hospital in Chandler," she said.

"Yeah, I bet cab fare from there would be cheaper."

And then I wanted to cry, because joking around with Josie felt just like it had in old times, only it wasn't. We weren't friends anymore. We had ruined everything over some stupid guy.

The Slurpee cup felt grimy, and I switched it from one hand to the other. "Look, Josie, I'm really sorry about our fight. I'm sorry about Ethan."

The smile dropped from her face, and she looked down. Her voice was only a little more than a whisper. "And I'm sorry I wrecked your chances with him."

"You didn't wreck them. He was only interested in me to make Ashley jealous."

Her gaze shot back up to me. "You're kidding? What a jerk."

"Yeah."

"We can do better," Josie said.

I nodded. "Right."

"Ted and Pete sounded nice. Too bad they don't really exist."

Which set me off laughing again. I stood there by the gas pump, time slipping away while Rebecca Lobo waited in an auditorium an hour and a half away, and I laughed.

Josie

After fifteen minutes of serenading gas station patrons, I was amazed anybody ever made a living as a singer. We went through four Celine Dion songs, a Smashmouth song—that was our biggest moneymaker because one lady said she'd give us five dollars if we stopped singing it—and a rap song that I made up as I went along, entitled, "Yo Man, I'm Stuck at a Gas Station." We jingled our Slurpee cup at anyone who came near the pumps and made a total of eleven dollars.

A young guy in a red Hyundai drove up to us, and I waited for him to get out of the car so I could start a second verse of our rap song, but instead he rolled down the window. "Are you Josie and Cami?"

"Yes." I had never seen him before, and I would have remembered. He didn't look much older than me, although he must have been at least sixteen to be driving a car. He had warm brown eyes, shaggy blond hair, and a tan that belonged on a surfer boy.

"I'm Daniel Dixon. Your friend Frederick called me, told me you were stuck here, and asked if I could give you a ride to Chandler."

I took a step closer to the car. "How do you know Frederick?" I asked. "And how did you get here so fast?"

"I live in Gila Bend. Frederick and I are in the same chess division. We play in tournaments together."

And then the name suddenly made sense. "Oh, you're Daniel the Knight Slayer."

He laughed and shook his head. "Um, right. Some people call me that." He looked from me to Cami. "Well, are you going to get in? Frederick said you were in a hurry."

I put my hand on the door handle, but Cami grabbed my arm away and eyed Daniel suspiciously. "How do we know Frederick really called you? Maybe that creepy gas station guy just overheard us talking to Frederick and told you about it, and you're planning to drive us out to the desert and hold us for ransom."

Daniel shrugged as though the accusation didn't bother him, then smiled at me. "Frederick told me when he sees you next, he has some really good jockette jokes to tell you."

I opened the front door of the Hyundai and slid in. "Frederick called him."

Cami handed me the Slurpee cup full of change. "I'll tell the gas station guy where we're going in case someone comes back for us and worries because we're not here."

"Yeah, tell him we're driving off with some guy we just met. That way no one will worry."

Cami didn't answer as she walked into the gas station. I stretched out my legs as I waited for her, avoiding a pile of CDs lying on the Hyundai's floor.

Daniel turned to look at me. "Fredrick came up with some really good jokes for you. Hey, how many jockettes does it take to plan a road trip?"

I leaned back against the car seat. "As if my day hasn't been long enough already."

"Two less than they started out with." Daniel laughed, then turned back around. "That was my favorite one."

Cami came back to the car to ask Daniel if he had a mobile phone. He did. She left that number with the gas station guy, and then called Frederick to thank him. At least she said it was to thank him; I think she was still worried Daniel might be an escaped criminal who prowled gas stations looking for victims, and she wanted to talk to Frederick just to make double sure it was safe to get in the car with Daniel.

Finally she got in the backseat and handed me the phone so I could talk to Frederick while Daniel drove. Frederick still hadn't gotten hold of Coach Melbourne's number, but he had tracked down the mother of one of our teammates' mobile phone number. She was on her way to Basha High and told him she would relay the message to the coach as soon as she saw her. Then Frederick made me listen to jockette jokes.

"Why did the jockette cross the road?

To chase down the car that just left her.

How many jockettes does it take to change a lightbulb?

Who knows? They can't count."

"Very funny," I told him. "How many chess players does it take to screw in a lightbulb?"

"I don't know."

"Neither do I, because no one ever watches chess players, because it's a boring game."

"Only to the uninitiated," he said. "I'll teach you how to play, and then you'll know what real competition is."

I glanced at Daniel and his surfer-boy hair. "Sure, you can teach me. Come to think of it, chess might be a lot of fun."

I said good-bye to Frederick and handed the phone back to Daniel with a smile. "You'll be staying to watch us play our game, won't you?"

He shrugged and smiled back at me. "I guess I could stay for a while."

"Great. I mean, I'm sure the coach, and the team, and my family will want to thank you for driving us all the way to Basha High. And by the way, if you see a five-year-old boy running around the bleachers and being obnoxious—that's Cami's little brother."

Daniel tilted his head. He had dimples and an adorable cleft in his chin. "You're not at all what I expected Frederick's friend to be like."

"What do you mean?"

"Well, it's just that Frederick's so . . . um . . . I mean, Frederick is a great guy, and everything . . . I just didn't think . . ." Daniel blushed, ran a hand through his hair, and stared straight ahead at the road again. "Never mind."

"No, tell me."

"Really, just forget I said anything." Daniel kept staring at the road, and I leaned back in the seat, wondering if I'd been complimented or not.

Daniel tapped a finger against the steering wheel. "You and Frederick aren't going out, are you?"

"No. We're just friends."

"Good," Daniel said.

And then I smiled. I'd been complimented.

We talked about Frederick, chess tournaments—which I suddenly found fascinating—and basketball. Daniel played some, but mostly he ran track. I found that fascinating too.

When we were half an hour away from Chandler, his phone rang. He answered it, then turned it over to me. It was Coach Melbourne, her voice coming between breaths of relief. "Where are you? Are you okay? Do you realize you nearly gave me a heart attack?"

"We're fine. We're about twenty miles outside of Chandler, and blame Ashley and Erica for the heart attack. They left us at the gas station on purpose."

Cami held out her hand as though she wanted to take the phone and add her own commentary, but I ignored her. I wanted to hear Coach Melbourne screaming at Ashley and Erica myself.

"Ashley already told me what happened," Coach Melbourne said. "She thought you switched cars to ride with Lucy. She told her mother you were with them, but the Simmonses didn't know anything about it, and so we only just found out you'd been left. Really, Josie, you girls should have stayed by the cars instead of dawdling around the gas station."

I clutched the phone harder. "We weren't dawdling. They tricked us into being left. Ashley told us you said everyone had to use the restroom, and then Erica told us to wait for Mikala, when Mikala wasn't even in the bathroom."

"I'm sure it was just a mistake, Josie."

I gripped the phone so hard I probably permanently indented my fingerprints into the plastic. "How could it be a mistake when we never said we were riding with the Simmonses?"

There was a pause. "You didn't talk to Lucy about going in her car?"

"No," I said, and then remembered I had spoken to Lucy in the parking lot. "I just told her I'd go by her car for a cookie."

"Well, Ashley must have misheard and assumed you were switching cars. Of course she should have double-checked, but *you two* should have stayed with the group instead of going off by yourselves."

"We didn't—" I started to say, but Coach cut me off.

"Look, this has been a bad trip all around, and I'm sorry you got left. We all are. If you could see how upset Ashley is about this, you'd know she didn't do it on purpose."

Yeah, I bet she was upset—upset we'd found a ride and wouldn't miss the game after all. But I wasn't going to be able to convince Coach Melbourne about her true intentions. I just had to be satisfied that Ashley's plan hadn't worked—and in fact had backfired in a way she'd never intended. For at least a little while, Cami and I were on speaking terms. I wondered if it would last, or if we'd soon be back to the prickly emptiness that popped up whenever we were together now.

I said good-bye to the coach and hung up, then handed the phone back to Daniel.

Cami leaned over the seat toward me. "Are Ashley and Erica going to be thrown off the team?"

"They told Coach Melbourne it was all a misunderstanding."

Cami grunted in disbelief. "And she believed them? She couldn't be that naive."

"Apparently she could be."

Cami sat back in her seat with a thump. "I sang Celine Dion songs to strangers at a gas station. Ashley and Erica have to have some sort of payback for this."

"A big payback," I agreed. "What should we do?"

"I can't think of anything horrible enough." Cami licked her lips. Her eyes narrowed. "Give me a little time, and I'll come up with something, though."

For a moment I tried to think of possible revenge scenarios, but I couldn't come up with anything that wouldn't get me suspended from the team.

I turned to Daniel. "What would you do?"

Daniel slid his fingers down the steering wheel. He didn't say anything for a minute, and I didn't think he'd answer at all. Then he said, "Do you know why I win at chess a lot?"

"Why?" I asked.

"I don't try to pay back people."

"What?" I said.

"If you're worried about retaliating against someone, you get caught up in the wrong game and lose sight of your goal. You have to decide which battle you want to win, and concentrate on that."

I ran my hand across the faded upholstery and felt the hum of the car on the road. "You don't think we should do anything to the girls who left us at a gas station?"

Cami humphed again from the backseat. "Well, now I know why I'm not any good at chess."

Daniel shook his head and gave a shrug. "I'm just saying it's better to think about things with your mind, not your emotions. If you react emotionally, you're likely to do something you'll regret later."

Like, say, telling the guy your best friend likes that she's a kleptomaniac.

Neither Cami nor I said anything for a couple of minutes, and I knew she was thinking about us. Everything we'd done lately, we'd done wrong.

Cami reached over the seat and picked up Daniel's MapQuest directions to the school. She studied them, then glanced at the clock on the dashboard. "We'll miss warm-ups, but hopefully we'll get there by game time."

What she meant was, "We'll be there when Coach Melbourne picks someone to play with Rebecca."

It had been such a competition between us, and now suddenly her name, just the thought of Rebecca, made me feel uncomfortable. I had been trying for MVP to bother Cami, and now it didn't seem worth it.

"It better not be Erica or Ashley," Cami muttered.

I tilted the Slurpee cup and watched the coins clang to the other side. "I hope Rebecca tells us what playing in the WNBA is like. That's all I really wanted to ask her. You know, whether basketball is still fun, or whether all the pressure turns it into work. Maybe you're always worried about being cut, or traded, or getting a lousy review in the sports section. Maybe the whole team goes back to the locker room and cries after they lose."

"Somehow I can't see Lisa Leslie crying."

"You're probably right. You know more about the players than I do."

It was a weak apology, and yet I hoped she knew what I meant anyway.

Fourteen

Cami

It was easy to tell when we'd reached Basha High. The parking lot was full of cars, a couple of them news vans.

Rebecca was here.

My parents and Josie's parents were waiting for us in front of the school. My parents were calm about the whole thing. They just gave me a hug, said they'd been worried, then patted my shoulder and told me to go dress down. Mrs. Caraway burst into tears, hugged Josie like it was her last day on earth, and swore she'd never let anyone else drive her anywhere again. She also said she would have a talk with Mrs. Holt, because as an adult it was Mrs. Holt's responsibility to make sure no one got stranded in the desert, and heaven knew what could have happened to us—we could have died—and if Mrs. Holt didn't have enough sense to make sure everyone was in a car, she shouldn't be allowed to drive students anywhere, and Mrs. Caraway was going to tell her so, and then after that, Mrs. Caraway was going to tell the same thing to Coach Melbourne and the school district.

Which almost made me feel sorry for Mrs. Holt, but not quite.

Inside the Basha locker room our clothes were waiting in our duffel bags. The rest of the girls were standing in a semi-circle in front of Coach Melbourne, getting a last-minute pep talk.

I hurried and changed, my heart beating fast and my fingers suddenly clumsy. Rebecca was probably out in the auditorium. How could anyone sit still and listen to the coach when Rebecca Lobo was somewhere near? She would meet us all. I knew she'd come and say hi to the team. Even though I knew this, had known it for months, I still didn't know what to say to her. What did you say to someone whose image had been plastered all over your bedroom walls for years? I wanted to stick out from the other three hundred people she would see today. I wanted her to remember me.

Josie finished changing before me and sat down behind the rest of the girls. I finally got my shoelaces to behave and joined her.

". . . so the important thing is that you represent your school well and have a good time. That's what playing basketball is all about." Coach Melbourne shifted the basketball from one arm to the other. "Now before I tell you who gets to play with Rebecca, I want you to know what a difficult decision it was. We've got a great team, and every one of you deserves it. You keep playing the way you are, and one day Rebecca may be asking you for your autograph." The coach gave a little laugh then, and probably we should have joined in, but we were all too nervous for laughter. "I could only choose one of you, though, so I chose the player who consistently, seriously, gives it her all every day. There are higher scorers and more visible team leaders, but there's one player whose extra effort affects our game on every level. She's an example to all of us. I chose Cami."

Coach Melbourne started clapping for me, and the other girls joined in, even Ashley, who looked like she wanted to cry. I took deep breaths, afraid in a moment everything would dissolve and I'd wake up in the front seat of the Holts' Honda with an impression of the car door on my face and find out every good thing that had happened this afternoon was just a dream.

Josie was talking to me again, and now this—I got to play with Rebecca Lobo. I turned to Josie, wanting to hug her, but she was just clapping calmly like everyone else, and I wasn't sure whether she was happy for me, or whether she wanted to cry, like Ashley, and was just doing a better job of hiding it. She hadn't won, after all. I had.

"Now let's get out there and play a good game!" Coach Melbourne said, then lifted her hand in the signal for us to yell, "Go, Sanchez!"

We gave our team shout and got to our feet to leave the locker room. I took hold of Josie's arm. We only had a few more moments before we got carried away in the events of the game. "You're the high-scoring player," I told her. "You're the best on the team. You deserve to play with Rebecca. I'm going to ask Coach Melbourne to choose you instead."

Josie's head jerked backward. "What? Are you crazy? She picked you."

"Yeah, but . . ." The other girls were going out the door. I knew we should follow them, but I still held on to Josie's arm. "When you wanted Ethan, I wasn't a friend to you. I need to be a friend to you now. I want you to play with Rebecca."

Josie blinked at me and spoke slowly. "No. When you had Ethan and I didn't, I wasn't a friend to you. I need to be a friend to you now. You earned the chance to play with Rebecca fair and square."

I hugged her then, all the hurt and doubt draining away. I was so happy to have her back.

"We're friends," I said.

"Friends," she agreed.

We went out to the auditorium, and started the game. To my credit, I did a good job of paying attention to the ball, as opposed to staring into the audience to see if Rebecca was watching me. I wanted to play the best game I had ever played. I wanted to sail across the court with the ball.

At halftime we were down by two points, but I didn't care. The team took seats on the sidelines while Rebecca stood at the podium, decked out in warm-up pants, a Connecticut Sun T-shirt, and Nikes. She gave a short speech about the importance of girls' sports to our health and esteem. She looked confident and at ease, like it didn't even make her nervous to speak while there were cameras right in front of her.

I agreed with everything she talked about, and couldn't remember a thing she said after it left her mouth. She looked like a movie star, like an angel—a really tall angel—and it seemed amazing she was actually in the same room with me. I was going to play with her. I was going to touch the same ball she touched.

"Now I'd like to do a little demonstration, and I need a helper from each team." She stepped down from the podium, and the coach motioned for me to get up.

"It's your time, Cami."

Next to me, Josie patted my back. "Don't trip."

But I wasn't worried about that. I jogged out onto the court feeling like I could fly. Cameras flashed all around me. I heard Caroline's voice somewhere from the stands yell, "Wahooo, Cami!" I was going to have to work with her on her sports cheers.

One of the Basha team members joined me out on the court, and we walked the last few steps up to Rebecca. She smiled at us, and I noticed she was prettier in real life.

"Ready to play, girls?"

We nodded.

"Don't show me up and make me look bad." I knew she was joking, trying to set us at ease.

"There's no way you could ever look bad," I said, and she gave me an extra smile.

"I like you already, kid."

Rebecca spoke to the audience, told them that we would demonstrate the layup, the jump shot, the free throw, and the three-man weave. It was all for show, really, since anyone who cared about basketball already knew these things, and those who didn't weren't likely to remember it just because of tonight. Still, I felt so important out on the court with her, running drills, passing the ball back and forth. All eyes, and several news cameras, were on us.

After she demonstrated the free throw, she threw the ball to me and said, "Your turn."

I held the ball in my hands, trying to be one with it. *I am the ball.*

Of course, telling myself I was one with the ball had never really worked before, so I held the ball close to my face and tried to send it psychic thoughts. "You like me. You want to go in the basket for me, just like you always do for Josie."

But I knew that wouldn't work either. I would make or miss the shot according to my own skill.

I aimed and flung the ball toward the basket, not breathing as it soared toward the backboard. It hit right above the hoop and dropped into the basket.

I breathed. I listened to the audience applause, and from the sidelines I saw Josie cheering for me.

Josie

A lot of people don't live up to your expectations when you meet them, but Rebecca did. She seemed happy to see us and to talk to us, even though we were a just a bunch of teenagers.

After her demonstration, the girl from Basha's team went back to the sidelines, but Cami paused there on the basketball court and said something to Rebecca—probably telling Rebecca what a fan she was and how she was naming her first-born child Rebecca even if it was a boy. And Rebecca took the time to talk back to her. (Probably telling her not to name her son Rebecca unless she wanted to see the kid beat up at recess every day.) For a couple of minutes the two of them talked out there on the court while the audience sat watching and waiting for the game to start. I bet most celebrities would have brushed off a kid who's trying to start a conversation in the middle of a full auditorium, but Rebecca didn't.

The news vans all packed up and left after Rebecca's demonstration, but she stayed for the entire game. Chandler was a tough team to play, especially since Ashley and Erica sat on the bench the entire night.

Which just went to show you Coach Melbourne wasn't as naive as we thought.

Any other day we probably would have lost to Chandler, but I had so much energy. Cami and I were back in our rhythm. I made basket after basket. By the end of the game Chandler had two guards constantly on me, and my game total was still fifteen points. When the ending buzzer rang, we'd won, forty-six to forty-three.

In the locker room afterward, Rebecca told us what a good job we did and gave us a two-minute talk about following our dreams. Then she handed out autographed pictures with the phrase "Keep on Playing" handwritten on the bottom—which I thought was utterly cool.

After that, she left with her husband, a tall, handsome guy with broad shoulders and a killer smile—which I thought was even cooler. It gave me more motivation to become an athlete. Athletes get to hang out with hot guys.

My parents did a lot of back-patting and congratulating me when I found them in the auditorium. "Great game. You played really well," Mom said. Another squeeze to my shoulder. A smile. A furtive glance at my father. "How do you feel?" I knew she meant about Cami's being chosen for MVP and not me.

"I'm glad Cami got to play with Rebecca. We're friends again."

Mom's face brightened. "You are?"

"Yeah, we made up at the gas station."

Dad took over the job of back-patting. "That's wonderful. I knew you'd work things out eventually."

Mom's gaze swung around the auditorium, searching. "A group of us are going to an ice cream place to celebrate. Why don't we invite Cami and her parents to come with us? There they are, over by those bleachers."

"Great," I said, then saw Daniel standing by the door. "I'll catch up with you in a minute, I just want to tell Frederick's friend thanks again."

I walked toward him, but halfway there Ethan and Justin intercepted me. They appeared out of the crowd, wearing Sanchez football shirts and big smiles. "Hey, Josie," Ethan said. "You were on fire tonight. Do you always play that well?"

"I try to."

He nodded at me, still smiling. "I came to see Ashley play, but I couldn't keep my eyes off you. You've got a great layup."

It seemed strange he was noticing me now, after all my failed attempts to get his attention. I wanted to tilt my head and say, "What gives? Are you trying to make Ashley jealous again, or did you just decide I'm cool enough to talk to now because you found out I'm good at basketball?"

"That's why she was so good at tossing grapes," Justin said. "She's had practice."

Ethan playfully swatted my arm. "We'll have to have a rematch. I still think I can beat you."

I returned his smile for the first time. "No, I'm done with that game. Besides, you probably shouldn't be talking to me, since you're going out with Ashley." And then, because I am more polite than Ethan, I waved good-bye to him and said, "See you around," before I walked off.

Daniel came up to me while I was walking toward him. His hands were thrust in his pockets. "There you are. Listen, I need to talk to you about gas fare."

Oh. I hadn't offered to pay him anything for making the trip to Chandler. I hadn't even thought about it, which now made me feel both stupid and ungrateful. How much did gas cost?

"There's eleven dollars in change in the Slurpee cup in your car," I said quickly. "And my parents can pay you more."

"No, that's not what I meant. They did pay me," he said. "And so did Cami's parents. Then a little while ago your coach gave me money even though I told her I'd already been paid." He nodded in Mrs. Holt's direction. "That lady over there insisted on paying me too. She gave me thirty bucks. I think she feels guilty." Daniel took his wallet from his jeans, unfolded it, and took out a wad of bills. "I can't take everybody's money. It didn't cost that much to drive here." He handed the bills to me. "How about I'll just keep the change in the Slurpee cup, and you can give everybody their money back for me."

Which meant that Daniel was not only cute, he was also honest.

I took a ten and a twenty from the wad of bills and

handed those back to him. "Keep Mrs. Holt's money. I'll feel better knowing you did."

He laughed, but took the money and slipped it in his wallet. "All right. I'll keep hers."

The rest of the bills felt like worn cloth against my fingers. I fidgeted with them while I tried to think of what to say next. I didn't want him to leave yet, but I knew he was about to go anyway. "Thanks again. I really appreciate everything, and I'll probably see you at the next chess tournament. I mean, you know, since Frederick and I are friends, and he's going to teach me how to play and everything."

Daniel smiled. "If you play chess anything like you play basketball, you'll be hard to beat."

I couldn't decide whether to say, "We'll see," or "I hope," so it came out, "We'll hope." Which didn't really make sense, but at least the sentence didn't contain the words *um, uh,* or *so.* I was getting better at this.

Daniel gave me another smile, and I thanked him again, and then we said good-bye.

My parents, Caroline, Cami, and her parents walked up. Cami's duffel bag was slung over her shoulder, and the spring in her step made her look like a professional. She gave me an innocent smile that was completely transparent. "Saying good-bye to Daniel?"

"He was refunding gas money. He said he got paid too much and asked if I could give it back to everybody."

I handed the bills to my mother, and she put them in her purse. "Such a polite young man."

"He should have kept it," Cami's mother said.

"We should invite him to eat ice cream with us," my mom said. "Do you want to run and ask him to come to Cold Stone Creamery with us?"

Cami giggled. I grabbed her arm before she could say anything to embarrass me, and we hurried out the door to see if we could catch Daniel. We ran out to the parking lot, and from a distance saw him walking toward his Hyundai. "Daniel!" I called.

He turned around, saw us, and waved. He didn't climb into his car. He was waiting for us to catch up to him so we could talk.

I slowed down to a walk because I was tired, and Cami matched my pace. And then I remembered the demonstration. "Hey, Camilla, I never asked you what you said to Rebecca Lobo out on the court."

"Oh, that." She smiled and slowed her pace even further. "I asked her if playing in the WNBA is still fun, or whether it all becomes work and everyone cries in the locker room when they lose."

"You asked my question for me?"

"Yeah. She says it's still fun even though it's a lot of work, and they only cry when Sue Bird starts singing along to the warm-up music."

"You asked her my question?" It seemed like the sweetest thing Cami had ever done for me.

I'd never been one to cry after a game, but that night I came close.

And not just because Daniel said he'd go to Cold Stone Creamery with us.

Fifteen

Cami

Basketball season ended better than it began. Our team won the final three games, probably because Josie and I were passing to each other again. For the last away game, we rode on the school bus, but Couch Melbourne still watched us like a hawk. It was almost as though she was afraid if she took her eyes off us, someone would evaporate.

Ashley and Erica never got suspended from school or barred from sports like I thought they should, but the coach didn't play them nearly as much as she had before, so she must have realized they weren't blameless. The rest of the players certainly realized it. It became a standing joke that if you didn't play well, the team would force you to ride in the Holts' car so you could be stranded somewhere in the desert.

Ashley got very snippy when we said those types of things, but I didn't care. It was almost like we'd impeached her as captain and as a result had more team unity. I was sad when the season officially ended and I had to turn in my uniform.

The only benefit was, I knew the next time I played school ball, I'd be playing JV or even varsity basketball. I imagined myself walking around high school with a letter jacket. I mean, how cool.

The science fair—or judgment day, as I called it—finally took place. We turned in our notebooks and boards, then during fourth period we went down to the gym to talk to the judges about our projects.

I wore my nicest khaki skirt. Caroline wore all her crystal necklaces in an attempt to invoke good chi at our interview. I'm not sure what the chi level actually was during our talk, but I'm pretty sure the judge's skepticism level was on the high side.

The woman wore a pained smile while she listened to us explain our experiment, and barely looked at the findings in our notebook. With a raised eyebrow she said, "You report that people noticed you staring at them fifty-eight percent of the time. That's a higher percentage than in Sheldrake's own experiment. How do you explain your results?"

Caroline fingered some of the crystals around her neck. "We may have greater psychic vibes."

"Or maybe," I added, "it's because we're two attractive teenage girls, whereas Rupert Sheldrake is an old guy who looks like he just crawled out of the spin cycle of a washing machine."

Caroline smacked me with her free hand, which I thought was totally uncalled for. After all, I was trying to sound scientific. I used the word *whereas*.

The judge asked us a few more questions, still with her eyebrow raised, and then moved on to the next group.

"Well, that's over," I said. "What place do you predict we'll come in?"

Caroline humphed. "You don't need ESP to predict we won't win anything. Pioneers of great ideas are never taken seriously."

Neither are pioneers of stupid ideas, but I didn't say this. Caroline and I had come to an agreement. I didn't make fun of her beliefs in ESP, and she no longer told me I had unresolved issues from a former life.

"Next year I get to choose our project," I said.

She rolled her eyes, which were decked out in lavender eyeshadow today. "You'll probably pick something totally mainstream."

Like that was a bad thing.

I stretched, looking around the gym at all the different booths. Over in the physics section, Frederick and Josie were talking to not one, but two judges. Frederick was animatedly waving a hand in the air, in what probably was supposed to look like a rocket flight. Josie smiled and nodded as she talked.

For sure, they were going to win something.

Of course, none of us would know the results of the fair until tomorrow. Apparently, going to school during the week wasn't hard enough, so the judges were making us come back on a Saturday to see whether our projects had been chosen to go on to the regional science fair. To make it worse, they wouldn't just tell us outright how our project had done. They put a slip of paper on the poster board that said "Winner," and then you had to go to the assembly later in the afternoon, listen to the boring talks on how we were the world's future, and wait to see whether you got first, second, third, or honorable mention in your category.

At least I wouldn't have to sit through all of that.

As we walked across the gym, I asked Caroline, "Are you even going to bother coming back tomorrow to see if we won something?"

A grin slid across her face. "That depends. Are you bringing your brother with you?"

Every time Caroline came over to my house, she and Kevin flirted with each other. I pushed open the gym door and shook my head. "How can you like someone who shoves his dirty socks into the couch?"

She shrugged. "He's cute."

"Yeah, and he consumes any and all junk food before I even know it's in the kitchen."

"Does he work out? He looks like he works out."

We walked down the hallway past rows of lockers and students who were avoiding going back to class. "For a Snickers bar, I'll tell you all of his secrets."

Josie

Frederick called me before I'd even finished getting dressed on Saturday. "We won something! Our board has a slip on it!"

Which was more than I had on. I glanced at my clock radio. "Is the school even open yet? Are you like the first one there?"

"No," he said indignantly. "The janitor is here too."

I sat down on my bed and pushed my pillows to one side to get more comfortable. "Great, Frederick, I'm glad we won something, but I'm not showing up at school until right before the assembly."

"Daniel is coming down to play in a tournament later on. He said he'd stop by the fair."

"Okay. I'll be there as soon as I get dressed."

Frederick laughed at me. He had no sympathy for my crush, which was unfair, considering he wouldn't even *talk* to Jessica Bing. At least I IM'd Daniel. He goes by NTslayer. Could anything be cooler? It made me think of a knight in shining armor up on a horse—a knight with surfer-boy blond hair. Daniel and I talk about school and sports, and he coaches me on how to beat Frederick in chess. Although even with Daniel's help, I've never been able to win a game against Frederick. Frederick gloats about that a lot.

I got ready for the science fair awards quickly. The rest of my family took much longer. My mother made my sisters and brother go, even though I could tell they'd all rather take a trip to the dentist than sit through a lecture discussing science fair projects.

Before the awards ceremony we walked around the gym looking at the other poster boards. Or at least my family did. I mostly looked for Frederick and Daniel, but didn't see either one of them.

Finally it was time to go to the auditorium. We shuffled into the room, taking our seats. I scanned the audience, but didn't find Frederick or, more importantly, Daniel. Maybe he hadn't come after all. I mean, who would want to waste their afternoon watching a bunch of strangers get science fair awards?

The room went dark, and I listened impatiently to the principal talk about hard work . . . innovators . . . cream of the crop . . . wave of the future . . . and so on. Jack was so bored he kept sliding off his chair onto the floor.

At last the principal turned the time over to Mr. Parkinson to give out the awards. He called students up to the stage and gave ribbons to the kids who did projects on the environment, computers, and engineering. Then he moved on to physics.

My mouth felt dry. My hands twitched against the armrests of my seat. It's only a science project, I told myself. It's just a ribbon.

Mr. Parkinson announced the honorable mention. Then third place. He still hadn't said my name. My heart beat faster. I gripped the armrests. He called out second place.

"And first place goes to Frederick Vine and Josie Caraway for Rocket Stability."

I stood up so fast the seat clanged behind me. I practically skipped to the stage.

Frederick was there before me, cool and collected, as though he won the science fair every year. Which perhaps he did.

We shook Mr. Parkinson's hand, and yes, I giggled, even though there has never been anything remotely funny about my biology teacher or shaking his hand. Then I went back to my seat, and Mom gave me a hug.

"We're so proud of you," Dad said, and Jack added, "Yay Josie!" even though he probably had no idea what I'd won.

I listened to the rest of the awards without listening. I just stared at the blue ribbon and gold lettering that read FIRST PLACE. Who would have thought such a short piece of material could make me so happy?

Afterward, I went back to the gym to gather up the poster board and notebook. Frederick and I hadn't discussed who would keep the stuff until regionals, but I figured I'd better make sure it didn't get left at school.

While I was going down the physics aisle, I ran into Frederick and Daniel. Daniel seemed taller and tanner than I remembered, but just as good-looking. Better, actually.

He smiled at me. I refrained from tripping.

"Congratulations," he said. "First place."

Frederick shrugged as we walked toward our table. "It's regionals we'll have to worry about. We didn't have much competition here." He stopped in front of one of the neighboring poster boards and waved a hand at it. "Jonah did one on quantum mechanics and the other worlds theory. What kind of project is that?"

Daniel flipped through the open notebook on Jonah's table. "Hey, don't make fun of the guy. In some alternate universe he's winning the science fair right now."

"Yeah, but never in this one."

Frederick and Daniel both laughed then. Which is the problem with having brainiac friends. You only get their jokes half the time.

Daniel smiled over at me again. "You'll do great at regionals."

I didn't know what to do with my hands, so I folded my arms across my chest; then because I thought that looked standoffish, I dropped them back to my sides. "Thanks. Frederick did most of the work."

Frederick tilted his head at me like I'd insulted him. "No, I didn't. You did half of it, except for those silly-looking glitter stars." He waved his hand in the direction of our poster board. "I didn't have anything to do with those."

I still felt uncomfortable taking much credit. "You had to teach me all about the center of pressure and the center of gravity."

"But you did a better job of talking to the judges." We reached our booth, and Frederick folded up the poster board. "Although you didn't have to tell them about the Scottish terrier attack."

"They thought it was funny."

"That's my point." He picked up the notebook and handed it to me. "Anyway, I think we make a good team." Frederick seemed to remember Daniel was standing there, because Frederick cleared his throat and added, "I mean, you know, in a *friend* sort of way."

Which was so obvious it made me blush, even though I

tried not to. I looked very steadfastly at the notebook, as though this was the first time I'd ever seen it.

Frederick tucked the poster board under his arm. As he turned to leave, it made a big sweeping motion across the aisle. "So Josie, at seven tonight I'm having some chess guys over to my house. You know, for chips, doughnuts, strategy techniques, that sort of thing. It would be a good place for you to come and practice your moves. Your chess moves, I mean."

I blushed again. "Oh . . . um . . . I'm not sure . . ." I glanced at Daniel to see whether Frederick's blatant matchmaking was making him uncomfortable or not. Daniel was smiling at me.

"You could bring along Cami and Caroline, if you want," Frederick added. "Are you in?"

"Yeah, I'm in."

My mother called to me from down the aisle, so I handed Frederick our notebook and told him and Daniel I'd see them later.

As I walked toward my parents I couldn't stop from grinning.

I was in.